DECLAN
&
BRAELYNN

WILLOW WINTERS
WALL STREET JOURNAL & USA TODAY BESTSELLING AUTHOR

From USA Today and Wall Street Journal best-selling romance author, W Winters, comes a provocative tale of a club designed for wealthy sinners. It's a story crafted for those of us who crave the villain.

I wish I'd known before it got to this point so I could have stopped it. I'd have chosen her above all else...if only I could go back. Even if it meant never getting to kiss her, to love her, to be consumed by the woman she is and the love she gave me. The only thing I know as truth now is that it's all my fault and it's all too late.

Her dark eyes hold obvious pain and misery, so much regret, but more than anything I know she looks back at me, her grip slipping, because she loves me.

She has no idea how much I love her, though.

This can't be how our story ends.

I'll burn the world down if that's what it takes. I'm never letting her go.

Then You're Mine is book three in the Shame on You Series. Tease Me Once and I'll Kiss You Twice must be read first.

"ALL THE DARKNESS IN THE WORLD
CANNOT EXTINGUISH THE LIGHT OF A
SINGLE CANDLE."

- ST. FRANCIS OF ASSISI

THEN YOU'RE MINE

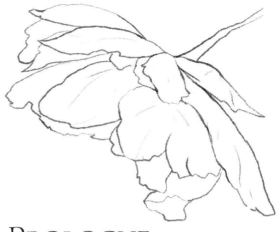

PROLOGUE

DECLAN

"Be my good girl and get down from there," I tell her, my voice is even and calm. Our gazes are locked even with the chaos erupting around us. The police scream. In my periphery, they dare to raise their guns at her. Rage and fear like I've never known consume me as she stares back at me.

Her wide eyes are glassy and her admission only minutes ago still rings clear in my mind. She was prepared to die before I opened that door. Death was her escape and the same resolution peers back at me. Drowning in sorrow, remorse, and in a pain I knew existed but refused to acknowledge.

"Now, my naïve girl. Get down from there," my voice lowers as I swallow thickly. My heart races and the pounding in my ears won't stop. She merely stares back at me, her dark eyes swallowed in sadness as she shivers with the incoming chill.

"I will never forgive you if you hurt yourself. Get down now."

A gust of wind blows through and I swear she sways just slightly. Her grip tightens on the windowsill, white knuckled, and yet it slips.

"Get down." I'm firmer as her gaze attempts to drift back to the open window.

She's only halfway there, a single step away from safety when they grab her. They pounce on her. Their hands on her small body is infuriating and yet, she's safe.

It takes everything in me not to fucking lose it. My breathing comes in shudders as I watch her being cuffed. She doesn't struggle, doesn't say a word, only looks up at me. While on her knees on the dingy carpet, her hair wild from the chilled wind, her face flushed, and doubt written in her expression, she waits for me.

My poor naive girl. What have I done?

"I'll fix this." I promise her softly, but I don't know if she's heard it over their demanding screams. Chaos surrounds us and I only wish I had the power to end it now. To be somewhere else in some other time where I can be the man she needs right now.

The cuffs around my wrists tighten and whoever the fuck is behind me attempts to pull me toward the door, but my feet are firmly planted.

It didn't have to be like this. None of it had to get this far.

"You're under arrest for conspiracy to commit murder, aiding, and abetting." They rattle off charges as she struggles to stand. Reality hasn't dawned on her. Not in the least.

She's still staring back at me, needing assurance. Needing help.

Why the fuck did I let it get this far? She's too good for this world.

Words tear up my throat, but as the two men behind me tug and shove me toward the door, their firm grasp on my shoulders, their attempts are too violent for me to resist any longer, I do what needs to be done. I protect her from them, but also from herself.

"You do not consent to a search and your lawyer is Michael McHale. Don't say a word beyond his name, Braelynn. Say nothing." My voice is firm as they pull her up, still in her nightgown and so small surrounded by three men in suits.

"Say it Braelynn; repeat what I just said." I call out to her as I'm pulled away. As they lead me down the narrow staircase of the shitty motel, I swallow down the words but then I call them out, hoping she can hear them.

"I love you! I'm going to fix this!"

CHAPTER 1

BRAELYNN

Declan's words repeat in the forefront of my mind, over and over, as I'm taken to the police station in the back of a cruiser. The smells of fresh coffee and stale fast food can't distract me from what he just said.

I love you. I'm going to fix this.

Emotions suffocate me to the point where even if I wanted to respond to the officers, I couldn't physically do it. I've spiraled, I've hit the hardest low I've ever felt, and yet... all I can think is that he loves me. Does he really love me? It wouldn't make sense for him to say it for any other reason... would it?

With my hands trembling in my lap, I hold them tighter and my body sways in the back of the car as we roll over a speed bump. My mind fills with memories of Declan. I can't stop thinking of his mouth on mine, his eyes, or his voice. I don't know how I'll survive with the thoughts that swim my head, much less how we'll get through this.

My gaze shifts to the front seat. To eyes that stare back at me. One of the cops is short and stocky, the other a thin woman with tired lines around her eyes. As time drones on, they talk shortly to each other. Neither of them says anything to me.

My thoughts are still racing by the time they park in the back of the station. The female cop pulls me out of the back.

With my arms pulled back and the metal biting into my wrists, it's far less than comfortable. She mutters something to her partner as he opens the large metal door and holds it so we can enter the station. Immediately, I'm assaulted with bright lights and stale white painted brick walls.

My heart races as I realize no one else is there. *Thump, thump.* It just doesn't feel right.

"Why aren't we going in through the front?" I dare to ask, speaking for the first time.

The female cop doesn't answer my question. It doesn't make sense, though. Why wouldn't they bring me through the front to the desk.

"I want to talk to my lawyer. His name is Michael McHale."

The other cop chuckles, deep and masculine. My heart races, faster than it did in the cruiser or in the motel. I've been through a lot of shit in my life, but that cop laughing because I want my lawyer scares the fuck out of me.

It's sobering and my reality comes in a sharper focus as our footsteps echo in the empty hall.

They pick up the pace and I follow, doing everything I can to stay calm. We're heading toward the front, I think, and it's loud out there. People talk over each other with cops barking orders and people arguing.

It's an odd sense of relief that floods me, but it's short lived as we never made it that far.

We stop outside a metal door well before we get to the lobby. He opens it and she leads me in. *Thump, thump.*

It's like the hospital all over again.

"I'd like to talk to my lawyer," I repeat calmly and once again I'm ignored.

"Stand here." Metal clinks and she uncuffs me. I swing my hands in front of me and rub at my wrists. Both arms are sore, though it wasn't long ago when I was cuffed at the motel.

"Thank you."

"Nothing to thank me for." She takes me by the arm and sits me down in a metal chair behind a metal table. One by one she cuffs my hands to the table. They're too tight and the cold metal bites into my skin. She checks them one more time, then turns to leave.

"I want my lawyer."

They both ignore me, and the door shuts tight.

I'm alone.

Fear floods in. I was mostly numb in the car, hell, I was numb before Declan walked through the door. But now I feel it all. And everything is breaking.

Every bit of me is breaking down and filled with regret. I wish I could just go back.

He said he loves me, and he said he'll fix it, but how? How is he supposed to fix anything? Hours ago I would have sworn he was going to kill me.

It's all just too late.

It's fucking cold in the room and the chill of it brings me back to the here and now. To a fresh new nightmare. The cops said things to me at the motel.

Conspiracy to commit murder.

Aiding.

Abetting.

I'm being charged, but...I don't understand why. Someone was supposed to explain it to me. I should be able to call my lawyer. I nearly call out again, demanding to speak to my lawyer. But I bite my tongue. They're watching. I know they are.

More emotions pile in and I find my hands shaking. I swallow again and again, not wanting to cry. I don't have control over my body, but I can keep myself from crying. Just barely.

How the fuck did any of this happen? How did I let it get

this bad?

A painful knot grows in my chest, but I refuse to let it take over. My body feels colder than it did in that tank of ice water.

The memory is chilling and again, I look to the door. With every small movement, the metal clinks on the table. Apart from the occasional jolt from the less than warm heater being turned on, the metal clinking is the only sound I can hear.

As I slowly slip, I know one thing is true. I wish I could call my mom. I wish I had talked to her.

It all feels hopeless, but if I could just talk to her, she would make me feel all right. Even though she'd know there isn't anything at all that's all right.

With a sudden bang, the door opens. Shocking me back to reality and startling the shit out of me.

Two new cops come into the room, letting the door bang closed behind them. I shiver in the gust of cold air. Both men, one clean shaven and the other with scruff. Neither of them give a kind expression as they stare at me so uncomfortably I have to look away.

It's as if they already know everything. Every little horrid detail.

Shame consumes me as one of them, the shorter one, puts a paper cup on the table in front of me. It's black coffee. The sharp aroma drifts up to my nose and goosebumps travel down my arms. I don't even like black coffee, but I'd appreciate the heat and something to help me think straight.

"That's for you," he says, then appears to notice that I'm handcuffed to the table. "Oh. Here."

He undoes one of the cuffs, letting my right hand go free.

I don't pick up the coffee. That's probably a trick so they can get my fingerprints on the cup. I don't have an ounce of trust for any of them. I don't know which parts of this are tricks. I put my hand on the table instead.

"Thank you," I murmur in response, staying calm as I can.

"You're welcome."

"I want to talk to my lawyer. His name is Michael McHale."

The second cop shakes his head. "He's not going to be able to get you out of this."

I almost say I didn't do anything. It would be so easy to say it and a nervous part of me wants to get it over with. But my teeth clench shut tight. Declan said to say nothing. Not a word except my lawyer's name. "Thank you" is more than he wanted me to say.

So I say nothing. The other chairs scratch on the concrete floor as they drag them where they want them and sit across from me. They ask me what I was doing there at the motel.

They ask me about the money.

They ask me about Declan.

I don't say a damn word in response. All I do is listen and watch their faces. They don't crack, they don't stop. Time ticks on in the too cold room and so much time passes that the steam from the coffee ceases to exist.

And it's colder. The room is so much colder now.

"You have to have something you want to get off your chest. It was very obvious that you would have done anything to escape him in that room." This statement is made from the taller of the two. Deep hazel eyes filled with what appears to be compassion stare back at me as I look up. Emotions swarm instantly and I could choke on them.

"Tell me what happened," the man attempts a comforting tone.

"I don't have anything to say to you." My voice cracks and I can feel the last thread stretching tight as I grip the edge of the table. I add, "Just like I told Detective Barlowe and Detective Hart at the hospital."

The cops exchange a confused look. For the first time since they entered, the air changes, their masks on their expressions fall. Pulling out a notebook, the shorter cop glances at me with that same confusion in his eyes. "You said detectives...who now? And when was this interrogation?"

Thump, thump. A chill runs down the back of my neck. Like that innate feeling that something is awful and so very wrong.

"I said I want my lawyer." I swallow thickly, glancing between the two of them who both look back at me with pinched expressions.

The other cop clears his throat. "There are no detectives with those names, but it is a tactic some criminal enterprises use to scare their men straight,"—he looks me up and down, and I'm glad that the table is covering most of my body—"or women. By faking an identity. Like two men on the Cross brothers' payroll acting as cops to see if someone would talk."

"Very common, unfortunately," the shorter cop agrees. "They likely lied to you to try to get you to fold. It's an effective way to add pressure."

My vision blurs and I struggle to stay calm.

I look down at the table and try not to move the wrist that's still cuffed.

There's no way he would do that to me. He wouldn't do that. He loves me.

The only person I believe is Declan. I don't trust these cops, and I never will. I can feel their eyes on me. I know they're being quiet on purpose so that I'll fill the silence. I want to. I want to speak so much that it feels like physical pressure in the room.

But Declan's voice comes back to me. *Don't say a word beyond his name, Braelynn. Say nothing.*

The charges come back, too. Conspiracy to commit murder, aiding, and abetting. I didn't help anyone commit murder. I didn't do anything. I repeat the words silently to myself. I didn't do anything. I didn't do anything.

A loud voice comes closer to the door and then it opens to reveal a man in a sharp suit who announces himself as my lawyer. He storms up with a scowl on his face and a briefcase slamming down on the table. "That's enough. These charges are bullshit and you know it. I'll be filing a harassment suit."

Although there's anger in his words, his tone is professional and even easy. As if it's already handled. As if I can get up right now.

"She's cuffed to the table?" The lawyer looks from the cuff to meet the cops' gazes.

"She was attempting to harm herself."

"No, I wasn—"

"Don't say another word," the confident lawyer with gray hair at his temples and simple silver-rimmed glasses tells me calmly.

He holds a hand up and waits for me to nod.

"You're interrupting an interrogation," the cop on the right says. "That's obstruction of justice."

"She was never even checked in." The lawyer crosses his arms over his chest. "Uncuff my client now or I'll push the issue."

"We need answers—"

"You needed to allow her to call her lawyer. That's the first rule you're supposed to follow. She's entitled to legal representation and I am certain she asked for it."

"We have a duty to conduct the interrogation before she's released on these charges."

"Have you filed them yet?" the lawyer asks. "Come on. Let me see the paperwork. Have the charges been filed?"

It's nothing like the lawyer shows on TV. A full-blown

argument ensues. One of the cops yelling over my lawyer who spouts off numbers of some jurisdiction or law. I don't know and I can't keep up. I just want to leave. I need to get out of here.

By the time the screaming match ends, my lawyer's face is reddened and any sense of calm professionalism is out the window.

"That's what I thought," my lawyer says. "Uncuff her. If you find the time to actually file these charges, then you can contact me directly. In the meantime, you can look forward to being served."

"This is an active case," the short cop points out, but it sounds like he's fighting a losing battle.

"It's an abuse of power, and you know that just as well as you know that these charges are bogus. Either book her or let her go."

The cops exchange another look. Lifting his hands, the taller one surrenders. I don't know what he's giving in on, but I hope it's letting me leave.

Everything happened so quickly, I don't think I took a breath through it.

The shorter cop stands up with a disgruntled sigh, leans over, and removes the second handcuff.

"This way, Braelynn," the lawyer says. He puts a steady hand on my elbow and steers me, silently, out of the room and toward the front of the building.

"I did ask to talk to you. They wouldn't listen."

"I'm sure you did." He doesn't slow his pace at all. "Don't worry, I've got you now."

We pass the booking desk, where a man is sitting in a plastic chair in handcuffs. He looks far too familiar. My world slows just then as his identity registers. Behind him, another man turns around and everything in me goes cold.

A camera flashes nearby, and there's another cop being booked.

They're the men from the hospital. Detectives Barlowe and Hart...my feet stop moving and I stare back as the man who just turned around, sees me, and quickly looks away. They weren't detectives. They're being booked. Oh my God. He did set me up.

The cops in the interrogation room were telling the truth. Declan lied to me. They were nothing but a test.

My stomach drops.

"Miss Lennox—" The lawyer tugs at me slightly, pulling me back to the present. I follow numbly, barely cognizant.

We head out into the lobby. Fluorescent lights shine down on yellowed linoleum by the front desk. Several people are sitting in plastic chairs, a couple of them having loud phone conversations. A female cop behind the front desk patiently explains to an elderly woman how to file a police report.

"Come on, Braelynn." My lawyer's tone is gentle, but he pulls on my arm. He must want to be out of here as much as I

do, but I slowed down. "I'll take you back to the house."

Fear paralyzes me. "Are they going to let you do that?"

He barks out a laugh. "Until they've filed charges, I'll do whatever I want. You need to get back to the house."

"Is Declan there?"

"Not yet," the lawyer informs me with a pat. "He will be soon though. Let's get you back."

Back to the Cross brothers and Declan isn't even there to protect me. Although at this point, I don't know if he would. I don't know what's real and what's a lie. All I know is that I need someone to help me because I am not okay.

Chapter 2

Declan

A full day I sat in a cell and all I can think about is her. I'm sick to my fucking stomach and on edge.

The holding cell is just an empty fucking interrogation room. The cold cracked cement floor is coated in dull gray paint. The steel bench is bolted down and the cylinder walls have texture but are coated in the same thick paint as the floor. It's empty and cold as ice...how fucking fitting.

There's nothing but the tick-tick-tick of the fucking clock that only seems to get louder.

The only conversation I had was with my lawyer who told me what I already know... They have forty-eight hours and no doubt they're doing everything they can to pin anything on me or get any warrants expedited.

Whoever signed off on this is fucked. I'll ruin them. I'm going to destroy not only them but everything and everyone they've ever loved.

My head falls back against the brick wall. I don't know if it's cold in here or if my body has just given up. I'm at war with myself. Fighting to not respond or react every time I relive what she told me and what she did. I've had twenty-four hours of remembering every moment. I could have saved her and walked away—to do the right thing by her.

I hate myself. That's truly what it comes down to. I fucking hate myself for what I've done to her, and all I want is to make sure she's okay and fix this.

My throat dries and my reddened, tired eyes go heavy.

They won't even tell me if she's all right. That's what I can't get past. I swallow thickly as I shove every emotion down and it's then that officers open the door.

I don't move or react other than to say, "I want my lawyer."

The metal chair groans against the cement floor as one of them kicks it toward me. It almost nudges against the bottom of my oxfords.

With the crack of my neck and the stiffening ache in my shoulders, I turn to look at him. Fucking bastard cops.

The short one is Angino and the taller one is McKinley. I recognize their names but not well enough. A file must've been slipped into someone else's hand. My jaw ticks as the two of them take a seat at the metal table.

The second I'm out of here, they're as good as dead and every pocket of the men on my side will be filled.

"Scarlet Miller."

McKinley talks as I slowly roll my shoulders, intending on sitting at the table if for no other reason than to look these men in their eyes.

As I stand, he babbles on, something about her family, her childhood. As if it matters at this point. As if a man like me could feel remorse for her. She set this into motion, didn't she?

It's all I can think as I pull out the chair and take a seat. I still can't figure out all the pieces, but I know she knew my poor naive girl was in too deep.

His voice gets louder, sterner, as his fist slams down on the table. "Got your attention now?" he questions. Angino's expression slips into a smug grin.

"What was that? I didn't hear you," I respond, and even though it's a prick response, it's also true. So I guess I'm an honest asshole.

"You knew she was undercover. You had her killed."

I hold his gaze for a good five seconds before reminding him of my lawyer's name.

"Why not Braelynn? She's a rat too." Angino says and I stiffen. I didn't know I could feel anger like this. With my brothers it's different. It's a fear, a sadness even. When the cops come for Braelynn though, all I feel is rage.

I swallow so fucking loud I know both of them can hear it. I've been in this room maybe twice. This specific room with my ass in this same uncomfortable chair.

I've been in other interrogation rooms maybe a dozen times, I've lost track. It was more often when we were younger.

I never gave enough of a fuck to give a reaction. Not until just now. It registers in their expression that just mentioning her name gets to me. There's an uptick in his asymmetric grin that confirms my intuition.

"My lawyer," I speak calmly and evenly although my pulse races in my ears.

Every inch of my skin singes and my muscles are coiled. Leave her alone. Leave her the fuck alone. Every time they mention her name, I'm all too aware I'm barely holding it together. I say nothing. Not a damn word as they press for more.

"We told her about Hart and...what was the other guy called?" The one asks the other and my throat dries out. He chuckles as I stare back at him.

Again, I give them nothing. Not a damn thing as they rattle on about how she's turning on me. How she knows I lied to her. How she almost killed herself because of me.

I hate them. I hate how much of the truth they know. The clock ticks and my blood pressure rises.

"I have your men under oath testifying that you killed two men to cover for your rat girlfriend."

Anger unfurls inside of me in a way it never has. How

dare they use that word with her name. *Rat*. The back of my teeth clench so hard they nearly break. Everything in me is exhausted and sore, everything dying to let it all out.

More importantly, betrayal ripples through me. Who did it? Who dared to call her a rat? I have no way of knowing if it's even true but in the pit of my stomach…I believe it is and it kills me. All of this is like a knife to my throat, as I slowly bleed out.

"They said you know she's a rat."

They poke-poke-poke, hoping for a reaction. They've certainly earned one but it will take time before I can follow through with recourse.

As my blood pounds in my ears, it takes everything in me not to say a damn word.

"They said she must be a good lay for you to turn on your brothers for her."

Just as I nearly snap and tell him to shut the fuck up and leave her alone, the door slams open.

"This ends now." My lawyer's voice is firm, firmer than normal. I'm all too aware that nothing about what has happened this weekend is normal. I swallow down every emotion, waiting for my lawyer to tell me to get up and follow him out. Just as he has every other time.

This time feels different though. It's heavier…

"We have forty-eight hours to hold–"

"You have a complaint filed against both of you on behalf

of several of my clients," McHale says sternly and that gets my attention. It's more than obvious that someone has changed the rules of the game, and we're only just now catching on to that. My lawyer's gaze never reaches mine. In a cold tone he adds, "I assume you're done here?"

CHAPTER 3

BRAELYNN

Michael McHale is kind on the surface, professional and quiet. He turns the heat up in his car, a top-of-the-line Lexus, but my body stays numb and shivers run down my spine. My throat is thick with shame and a confusion I can't seem to shake loose. Outside the car, everything blurs and time passes too quickly; there are streetlights every so often. Blocks go by in darkness. Some houses have lights on, and I wonder about all those people living different lives. People lie to each other all the time, which is to be expected.

Declan wasn't supposed to lie to me.

If there's real love there, if he truly loves me, then why does he lie to me?

I'm glad to be away from the jail, but all too soon the

lawyer pulls into the driveway in front of the house and I'm reminded of the fear.

"I'll help you out." A protest nearly rises to my lips. Somehow it seems like it would be better if he just drove me around until I could figure things out. I don't trust any of my own thoughts though. I don't know what's real or what's going to happen to me when I step through those doors.

There's no way to figure it out without speaking to Declan, though. I've faced worse things than a conversation, but it feels like the ground has been forcibly moved under my feet.

I wouldn't mind falling asleep in the car and waking up where nobody knew my name, and all the secrets and lies were far behind me. I wouldn't mind if I forgot it all. Every reason I had to just jump. To start over. My head falls back as I try to remove that thought. I don't want to die. I turn my gaze back to the house, but I also don't know that I want to go back. I'm trapped and I don't know what's right or wrong anymore.

If I left now though, I'd never find out why Declan lied, and I'd never find out if he really loved me, and I'd have to live the rest of my life not knowing.

That hurts more than anything else. I still don't exactly want to get out of the car when the lawyer opens the door and waits expectantly.

"Thank you."

The lawyer keeps his hand above my elbow on the walk

to the front door, more than likely because my legs wobble, and I'm sure many of my thoughts can be read on my face. My heart races. The truth is behind that door, somewhere. It's a matter of getting Declan to give it to me, and if he doesn't... that means our love is a lie, too.

The lawyer knocks lightly on the door, then opens it without hesitating. It's not locked. They're waiting for us.

We step inside.

A false sense of relief washes over me, but it's quickly replaced by the cold, numb feeling I had before. Carter's waiting for us near the front door with his arms crossed over his chest and a serious look on his face. Declan is nowhere to be seen.

Shivers run down my spine as my gaze drops down the crisp suit and lands on the floor. Breathing is harder feeling his eyes on me.

"Where is Declan?" I manage to whisper to the lawyer, my hand rushing to land on his and keep Carter from holding me. But he doesn't allow that. He slowly lets me go in the grand foyer of the estate. Handing me over to Carter Cross.

"He's still waiting to be released."

"Michael, what is the update?" Carter questions businesslike, without addressing me at all.

The lawyer clears his throat. "Maybe we should discuss this in private?"

Carter nods sharply.

"Lead the way." The lawyer steps further into the house as my feet remain planted where they are, the door to my back. Once again I'm wondering if I could possibly open it.

Carter begins to follow the hollow steps of expensive shoes against marble, but he hesitates. "Do you need company?" His question is gentle and catches me off guard so much that I peer up into his dark gaze.

I shake my head as I swallow thickly. Without conscious consent, my arms cross over my chest and then I let them drop again, all the while avoiding his monitoring gaze. I've had enough of being scared and confused, and it's not getting better. But all I know for sure is that I want Declan.

Eyes guarded, Carter looks me up and down. "Where will you be?"

My voice cracks, so I clear my throat and start again. "Kitchen."

He nods, then holds out a hand and gestures toward the kitchen.

A light above the stove is on, giving low light to the space. Time passes so slowly and at first I sit, but then I stand and go about without thinking much. I open cupboards until I find a glass, then fill it in the sink. The cool water eases my dried throat, but it makes me feel a bit sick. I press my wrist to my forehead and make myself drink more water. When the glass is half-empty, I dump the rest into the sink and put the glass down harder than I meant to. I almost expect it to crack, but the glass holds.

It feels less fragile than I do. The kitchen begins to tilt, and damn—if I don't sit down soon, I'll probably fall and hit my head on the floor. Then I'd be at the mercy of whoever finds me.

I get to a chair at the kitchen table just as my knees go wobbly and give out. Burying my face in my hands, I feel them shake. Memories of the hospital and the two fake detectives make me feel sick and betrayed. By those two men, for playing a role like that and asking me so many questions, but mostly by Declan.

He lied. It's all I can focus on because I don't want to believe it. I remember how he kissed me while I laid in that bed. How he silenced every fear just then.

How much of it was a lie?

Though the lawyer and Carter aren't speaking loudly, I can hear the murmurs of their conversation through the walls. I didn't want to be alone, but this is the worst way to be alone. I'm not by myself. I'm with Carter, who I know is going to watch my every move, and I'm not protected.

I swallow thickly as the memories of feeling so safe with Declan rush back into my mind. My eyes burn but I don't let any tears slip down under my palms. Was I wrong to believe he loved me? It seems from all the evidence the day has revealed that I was.

The refrigerator kicks on, humming away in its spot in the kitchen. Thankfully it blocks out the rumble of Carter's conversation with the lawyer. I don't want to hear a word of it. I don't want to be a part of any of this.

I breathe through my nose and release each breath through my mouth, trying to calm myself. Whatever else happens, I need to stay as strong as I can.

Voices in the hallway tell me that Carter and the lawyer are finished talking. I hear them exchange goodbyes, and then the whoosh of air as the front door opens. It closes a second later and I hear the lock flip.

Then footsteps. Fuck. My heart thumps at the same pace.

I take my hands away from my eyes and sit up straight behind the table. I could pray and beg for that man not to come in here but I know he's going to. Of course he is.

Carter enters the kitchen with worry in his eyes and comes to me without hesitation, putting one hand on my shoulder. "How are you doing, Braelynn?"

It's not at all what I expected to happen. An interrogation would be more in line with what's happened since the police burst into the hotel room. The unexpected kindness from Carter makes me want to let go of all the strength I've been holding on to and break down. My chin quivers, but I close my teeth together. If I let the breakdown happen, he'd hold me.

"I'm okay." At my words, he squeezes my shoulder and moves to the other side of the table, sitting down across from me.

I can't help but ask the worry that never leaves me, "Is Declan going to be all right?"

Even asking the question makes me feel a hundred times more conflicted. If he doesn't love me, then I shouldn't care. But the feelings I have for him can't be turned on and off with a snap of my fingers. Heartache gets stronger in my chest until it seems almost impossible to avoid breaking down.

Carter must be able to see that because his expression is genuinely worried. "He'll be fine. I'm concerned about you."

He's quiet, and my first thought is that I shouldn't say anything. Or that I should say I'm fine. I war with myself internally and I know too much time has passed when I settle on the truth.

"I don't think I'm okay. I don't trust myself." My hands shake on the table and I thread my fingers together and hold them tight. The storm of emotions inside me only gets stronger. If I had the freedom to cry and let it all out, maybe I'd feel better...or maybe not. It's hard to tell if I have any freedom at all. I meet Carter's eyes across the table. I don't know what he knows. "Do you know what happened?"

"We know everything." The way he says it and the look in his eyes...

This truth makes my stomach feel cold with all the dread of the day. It gets colder and colder until finally it goes numb.

They know everything.

There. That's out in the open.

I swallow thickly, my mouth dry, and brace myself for the next question I have to ask him.

"Are you going to kill me?"

I shouldn't be afraid, death would at least be an escape, but fear runs through me, coating every vein in more cold. I stare down at my hands on the table. Men like Carter could kill me in a second. That's also true of Declan. If that's their intention, I probably won't have long to worry about it. It could be over in the time it takes to pull a trigger.

But I am afraid. *I don't want to die.* Regret leaves a bitter taste in my mouth and my chest hurts more than ever.

"Braelynn."

I look up at Carter's face and from his expression, I think he's said my name several times. The question I asked hangs between us. Are you going to kill me? I sit up straight and steel myself for an answer. Carter doesn't look like he's about to pronounce a death sentence, but I've been wrong before. I've been so, so wrong before.

"We're not going to kill you." His voice is low and steady, not shaking at all, though I don't know why it would be. He's used to things like this happening.

"Okay." I can't help the relief that trickles through my veins. It's probably foolish to be relieved at a time like this, but I'm not in charge of my body that way right now. Then again, there are worse things than dying, which crashes through the relief like a boulder. "What are you going to do to me, then?"

Carter looks me dead in the eyes. "We're going to keep you safe."

CHAPTER 4

DECLAN

Sleep weighs my eyes down as the car door opens in the crisp cold. I take my time getting in the front and sink back into the leather seat as Jase drives off. Nothing seems real. Yet everything is heavy. I can't stop thinking about my Braelynn.

For hours on end, I've tried to decide what to do to make it right. But I don't know how the fuck it got so bad. The vision of her in the window is one that's stayed with me.

I know she loves me. I fucking know she does. But then how could she possibly want to end it? I don't understand. All I know is that I'm not okay and neither is she.

Jase asks me something and I barely hear it. I shrug, not wanting to stop for anything. I just want to get back so I can hold her again. I don't know what to say to her though.

Everything I've done has made things worse.

"Are you all right?" Jase asks and again I shrug.

I don't trust myself to speak. All the while in that holding cell I held it together, but it doesn't escape me that without them watching, all I want to do is break down.

"What the fuck happened in there? Did you tell them something?"

My eyes narrow as I stare back at Jase. Anxiousness is rolling off his stiff shoulders as he glances between me and the road.

"As if I'd ever fucking do that," I answer, my voice low. The anger and disappointment are apparent.

"Don't fucking look at me like that," Jase answers, relief more evident than anything else. We slow to a red light and he questions me again, "What the hell happened then?" Worry riddles into his words.

I swallow thickly, refusing to look back at my brother as the memories of what she almost did play back in my mind.

"Carter didn't tell you?" I ask him as I stare at the window and the car ushers forward again. My throat is tight and my voice nearly cracks, "He didn't tell you what happened?"

Silence from my brother brings my attention back to him. He doesn't look back at me as he drives, his hand twisting on the leather steering wheel. He adjusts in his seat and takes in an audible breath but still doesn't say anything.

"He had to have told you," I press him, not wanting to be

the one to say it out loud again. I don't want to breathe more life into it. I want it all to die and wither away, never to be thought of again.

"Which part?" Jase questions, gently and carefully. When he looks back at me all I see is pity.

"The part where she asked me to kill her in her sleep?" I question him with tears pricking at the back of my eyes. "Or the part where she almost killed herself and jumped out the fucking window?" My voice raises as my hands tremble.

I'll never forget that sight. I'll never forget the way it felt to hold the woman I love, while she held me back with everything in her, relieved to be done running and accepting of her death.

So long as I live, she shouldn't have those fears. She shouldn't have those thoughts.

Tears escape and I angrily brush them away at my brother's silence. "Well did he fucking tell you?" I nearly scream at him, the anger more my friend than the sadness that sinks it's claws into me.

Jase's response is gentle again, "Yeah, yeah he told me what the lawyer told him and what you told the lawyer. We all know." Jase's shoulders relax somewhat, his tone is comforting when he looks back at me. "I know it can be hard when there's tension between you and the person you have feelings for–"

"Tension?" Indignation ricochets in the cabin of the car as

I yell out. "Tension?"

Jase looks out the window and when he looks ahead, I can see it in his face. "What do you want me to call it, Declan? What do you want me to say?" he asks and it's obvious he's not doing well with it either. Then it hits me.

"You tell Bethany?" I ask him and he better fucking not have. No one else needs to know. For the love of God, it all just needs to go away.

"Yeah," he admits.

"What the hell?" I kick back in my seat wanting nothing more than to get out of the fucking car.

"I had to!"

"Had to?" I can barely look at him when he looks back with that look in his eyes. Bethany is his wife, but she's also worked in a psych ward.

"She might need help," he says, as if it's that easy. As if there's a pill that can take all those thoughts away.

"Like a fucking pill? Like being admitted?"

"I didn't say that," he answers.

"She was perfect and I ruined her," I say the truth out loud. If she'd never met me, she'd be happy and loved. Some nine-to-five bastard would have loved her right. He would have never let anyone hurt her. He wouldn't have let her think those thoughts.

I'm not ashamed to let it all out, my body shaking as the tears spill.

The tires squeal as Jase pulls over, his seatbelt clicks off and his hand is on my shoulder as he tells me it's going to be all right. How the fuck could it possibly be all right when I don't even know what to say to her? I'm afraid I'm only going to hurt her more.

CHAPTER 5

BRAELYNN

Carter said they would keep me safe, but in the bedroom with the door closed, I don't feel safe at all.

There's a mix of nervousness and something else. Something I can't place. I don't know what I feel. The room is warm. It's clean. It's a room I know all too well and one that holds both good and bad memories. I don't have the feeling anyone is going to rush in and arrest me. That's better than before, at least. I sit on the bed and turn the screen of my phone on and off again. Checking for a message from him.

I just need him here.

Closing my eyes, I inhale deeply. The room smells like him. His clothes are in the closet.

I'm all too aware that I can't call anyone. I can't see anyone.

I'm a prisoner all over again.

I don't know what to do or if I even should do anything. It's easy in a way to simply not think and be a prisoner.

My body is tired and a little numb. It takes more effort than it should to go to the pristine bathroom, brush my teeth, and wash my face. I go through the drawers of all the clothes Declan bought me, although none feel comfortable and many are still confiscated in the duffle I took to the hotel. Instead, I settled on an undershirt from Declan's drawer. I change and get under the covers.

I could call the cops, but I don't want to. It doesn't make much sense, anyway. The police aren't on my side.

I could choose someone else to tell, but I don't want to do that either. My mother comes to mind and it all hurts all over again. I don't want to drag her into this. I could never forgive myself.

I'm trapped. That's what this feeling is. I'm trapped and worst of all, I'm doing this to myself. I'm lying here thinking of things I could do and refusing to do any of them. I'm just giving up. I can't blame myself or feel any sense of shame either. There's some part of me that wants to be in Declan's bedroom no matter what.

At least I'm safe here. Safe from everything other than my own thoughts.

With my throat tight from that thought, I close my eyes so I don't cry. I don't want to do that, either. It would probably be best if I didn't. Crying wears me out, and I need to be ready for whatever comes next.

The heat clicks on in the room and it's the first sound I've heard since I've lain here.

What comes next? I don't know. I don't know anything anymore. Carter's not going to let me leave. I don't know how long the promise to keep me safe will last. I don't know if he and his brothers mean it. The only thing I know is that I need Declan to tell me everything is going to be all right.

At that thought, the bedroom door opens. It startles me in the bed and I jerk upright with a racing heart, pulling the covers to my chest.

It's Declan.

I'm instantly nervous. Instantly relieved. My hands are shaky and my mouth is dry. For a few seconds he stands at the door and stares at me. Wrinkled shirt and all, he's still handsome and the sight of him makes my heart beat faster. His dark eyes search mine as my pulse quickens.

Say something.

This is the first time we've been in the same room since I thought he was going to kill me for betraying him. My chest hurts when I think about what I was prepared for and what I expected to happen.

Tears prick and I sit up straighter, moving slightly to give him room if he wants to sit.

What is he going to say to me? What is he going to *do?*

Everything is different, but nothing has actually been fixed. Declan and his brothers know what I did. They know the truth, but that doesn't mean I'm better off.

I'm torn between guilt, shame, and fear. I bounce between the emotions, and I keep landing on one thought in particular—*how did this happen? How did I get to this place?* Nothing turned out the way I thought it would.

The silence gets heavier as his eyes travel down over my body. He can't see much of it with the blanket covering me. Letting out a breath, he breaks our gaze without a word.

Only then does he turn back to close the door.

Now we're really alone. Heat runs through every inch of me. Both in fear and in want.

He faces me again and runs his fingers through his hair. Declan came in here ready for anything it appears. My heart beats heavy and hard imagining what must have been running through his mind. Now that he knows I'm alive, he looks exhausted. He shakes his head a little and strips off his shirt. He throws it into a hamper in the corner of the room.

"Declan?" I whisper his name.

"I have to ask you some questions." There's emotion beneath the surface of his voice. He's not able to hide it very well.

I pull the blankets in tighter. "Okay."

"What did they offer you?" The question hangs in the air.

"Who?"

"The cops." Declan undoes his belt and takes his pants

off. He pulls the belt through the loops and tosses it into the opposite corner. It lands on a chair. The pants go into the hamper, too. He glances at me to see if I have an answer.

I shake my head.

His brow furrows. "The feds?"

"Nothing," I manage to say through the knot of emotion in my throat as he continues undressing down to his boxers.

Declan crosses to the bed and climbs in next to me. The bed groans with his weight. He settles close enough to me that his warmth welcomes me to come closer. Once he's under the covers, my heart does another flip. The tension between us feels thick enough that I could almost pick it up and touch it.

He must feel it, too, because he rolls over to me with a low noise and props himself above me on his elbows. It's a sexual position. I can feel how hard his body is through his boxers. But his eyes are deadly serious. My heart rampages in my chest. All I want in this moment is for him to tell me it's all going to be all right—like he did back at the hotel when I was arrested.

Declan strokes a lock of my hair away from my face with a gentleness I've never known from him. He murmurs in a pained voice, "Don't ever do that again."

Whatever emotion he was trying to hide before isn't hidden anymore. His voice is rough, as if he's been shouting. I ask in a cracked voice though I already know what he means, "Which part?"

"The part where you tried to take yourself from me."

Declan's serious expression falters, and the corners of his mouth turn down. His glassy eyes warn me that he's going to cry. That look on his face makes it even harder to breathe. I open my mouth, but Declan swallows hard and continues speaking before I can say a word.

"I don't care how bad it gets. I love you, and it's never too late. You hear me? It's never too late, and I can always fix it. I'll fix this." He tells me words I could only dream of. The ones I've been praying to hear. Promises that break every wall I've built, no matter how shittily they were cemented together.

Tears make my throat close. I've wanted this to be fixed for so long, and it doesn't seem like it'll ever be possible. I ask the unspeakable, "How?"

"I'm still working that out." He swallows so loud I can hear it. "Just stay here with me."

He nudges my nose and even though that piece of us is mending, the lies and what drove me to the edge are screaming for me to say something. To do something, right now. And not to wait.

It would be easier just to go along with it, but I can't. I'll never forget how I felt at the police station when I realized what Declan had done. He sent people to pretend to be detectives. He set up a test for me. So whatever he says now about loving me and fixing things, he can't be trusted.

"You lied to me."

His face falls and his forehead leans down to touch mine. It only lasts for a second and he picks his head back up to look into my eyes. "I lie to myself sometimes, too."

"I don't—"

Declan silences me with a kiss. It's a deep, desperate kiss, and it contains all the emotion from his voice.

If I were a stronger woman, I'd shove him away. But I need this as much as he does. I realize that's where the tension was coming from. It's taken him over, and it took me over, too. I put my hand to his chin to feel his rough stubble and kiss him back with the same desperate need.

I kiss him like I trust him again. I know I shouldn't do that. I should keep looking for a way out. A way to fix this myself. I know better than most that you can't rely on anyone else in life, no matter how much you want to.

For now, though, I can't do anything but press myself closer to him and kiss him harder. My back arches and I brush myself against him, needing to feel him.

I need this. I need *him*.

Declan makes a low noise into my mouth and pulls back, breath catching. "I'm going to fix this." The tone of his voice is so serious that I know he means this as a promise. "I will never hurt you...even if you leave me. Even if you don't love me, Braelynn, I love you." He murmurs his promises into the crook of my neck between opened mouth kisses and I fall. I fall for every word, for everything that this man is.

Before I can say it back, his mouth is on mine. Declan's body moves and I spread my thighs so he can get between them. I would have missed this so much if they'd kept me in jail. I would have missed losing myself in the sensation of pleasure that just touching him brings me.

He kneels up between my thighs and strips off his boxers. I don't see where they land because all I care about is bringing his body back to mine. He leaves a little room between our hips so he can reach down and stroke me.

He groans, "I need you," in a deep masculine throaty sound that makes me all the more ready for his touch.

I don't even make an attempt to say it back. I show him by wrapping my arms around his neck and pulling him down to me. He grips my hip and angles me up so he can take me with one powerful stroke. Which he does effortlessly and my head falls back, my mouth falling open. He doesn't stop, he kisses me all the while with every needy stroke.

That's when the tears come. I bury my face in his shoulder and work my hips against his. All I want is our pleasure. There's still so much to face outside this room. I don't want to think about any of it. I can't. I'm too tired and needed this too much. I needed him to say what he said.

If he loves me, we can figure out the rest. Cause I'll be damned, but I love him too.

He grips the headboard with one hand so he can fuck me harder. Our gazes lock while he takes me, his other hand coming up to grip my chin.

Declan changes his angle so my clit gets more contact. The pleasure in my nerves makes it too hard to think about everything that's happened. It takes me to my safe place.

"Yes," he says, and I realize a few seconds later that it's because I'm going to come. Pleasure rocks through me so intensely that my toes curl.

I can't think much of anything when he kisses the side of my neck. Declan stays inside me while he wipes the tears from my cheeks.

"I'll fix everything," he promises again. "Don't cry."

I don't say anything because I can't promise I won't cry. I probably will.

CHAPTER 6

DECLAN

I swear to God that fucking grandfather clock in the corner of Carter's office has the loudest fucking tick. My brothers take their seats—Carter behind his mahogany desk with the curtains drawn behind him, Jase to my right in the wingback chair that matches mine and sits across from Carter, and Daniel by the fire, staring at it rather than us. The fucking clock ticks away, reminding me of how quickly time moves.

How mercilessly it takes from us. There's never a moment of silence.

The fire crackles and snaps, the heat brushing against us as Carter pours a glass of whiskey into his crystal tumbler.

He offers the bottle to Jase, who declines. Daniel takes him up on it, pouring a glass for himself then a second one for me. *Fuck it.* I stare at the amber liquid for only a moment before downing it, letting it burn all the way down. The tumbler hits the desk a little too hard, but that doesn't stop Daniel from pouring me another.

Carter nods slightly before taking a heavy gulp. Jase grips my shoulder and then tells Daniel that he'll take one too.

We've had hard days, hell, we've had difficult years. Tonight is not one of them, yet it feels the heaviest.

"She didn't say shit, and they don't have anything on her," Carter finally starts.

"I know," I peer up at him and spit out the one thought that won't let go of me. "She never said anything to anyone."

My brother looks at me but doesn't comment. Jase and Daniel don't have anything to add either. A heat pricks at the back of my neck and I can't help but rub it and then readjust in my seat.

"What do you think of her?" I barely manage to get out. Half of me doesn't care. I want her, I love her. The other half of me desperately wants them to love her too. I need them to. To protect her and be there for her if something does happen to me.

I've always been there for the women they love. They're family.

I need Braelynn. I need her in my life and even if I'm no good for her, now she needs me too.

"She's scared."

"We already knew that." Daniel tells Carter as he takes a seat on the ottoman in front of the fire.

"I think she's less scared than before." Jase offers.

I nod, listening and knowing, although that's not what I meant. I have to bite my tongue not to ask them questions they've asked me before. Questions like: do you think she loves me? Do you think we'll be all right?

Instead I clear my throat and add, "She's definitely better than she was." I grip the crystal tumbler and swirl it gently, watching the liquid twirl in the glass. "She's loyal," I add, talking over Jase who started saying something. "She may be scared but she's loyal. She'd rather die than upset me," I tell them and the pain ricochets in my chest.

I hate myself for it. For everything I've done to her.

The agony that hasn't left me tightens its grip and it feels like I can't breathe.

Thankfully, Jase offers a solution to the problem at hand. "Shotgun wedding?"

"She won't be forced to testify," I state clearly, very much anticipating the answer they'd have.

"It needs to be done immediately," Carter says and I nod.

"Paperwork can be done in forty-eight hours according to McHale's contact."

"I haven't discussed it with her yet, but she'll do what I ask of her."

It's quiet and I wonder if my brothers question whether

or not she will go along with it. It fucking guts me and I don't have the balls to ask them. I already feel as if I'm at death's door and I don't want to know the truth.

"Once that's taken care of," Carter pauses, his gaze falling on me, "we won't have anything to worry about on that front, right?"

"She's not going to say anything. I don't think she ever did." I push the issue once more. It wasn't her that leaked to Scarlet. I fucking know she didn't do it.

Jase glances at me from his periphery, his brow arching too much for my comfort.

"There's a rat somewhere in that bar; it's not her though," I tell them and stress it, my voice cracking.

"All that matters right now is getting you both the paperwork so the feds leave her alone." He breathes out heavily before asking, "I imagine she has an idea of what she's agreeing to?"

It's a blow to my chest. They might protect her, but it's only for me.

I have nothing in me now to fight or to argue. "Marriage is a contract and she understands the terms," I tell them.

I'll take care of her in every way she needs. I will carry every burden and love her in every way I can. And she'll stay by my side...whether or not she wants to.

They'll get to know her. We'll figure out the truth. Or else I don't know what will happen once all of this blows over.

My throat tightens when I add, "It's not like she has much of a choice."

My brothers are quiet. I wish they'd fucking say something.

"Is she okay?"

"No." I put it bluntly and when I do, everything feels as if it tumbles out of me. "I wish I'd never touched her. She doesn't deserve this."

"No you don't." Jase leans back, huffing a humorless laugh. "We're all too selfish to wish for something like that," he murmurs and then, and only then, does he look at me. "All love is selfish."

"Just make it better. Make it right and it'll be okay," Daniel tells me and his expression is sincere.

"I don't know how to make it right in the ways that matter." Carter opens his mouth to say something but I cut him off, "But I know there's hell to pay and I want the fucking station to run red with blood."

Carter's lips slip into an asymmetric smile.

"I'll happily help you there," Jase says with a grin.

"Let's start with that fucking detective," I tell them and they nod, "he'll lead us to the rat." They don't stop nodding in agreement and for the first time I feel slight relief.

"Ransack his office? Beat it out of him? What are you thinking?" They ask and I answer, "I'm thinking I have a lot of pent-up anger right now, and there are a lot of pricks I can take it out on. I'd like to do that personally and I made a fucking list."

CHAPTER 7

BRAELYNN

I wake up to a soft noise in the room. At first, it's gently pulling me from slumber...but then I remember.

My eyes snap open. The covers are pulled up tight around me warm and comfortable, although my heart is racing. *Declan's room.*

The sound happens again.

I turn over and push myself up on my elbow. It's early. The sun coming in through the windows is only just starting to come up, but Declan stands near the closet. He has pants on already and pulls a T-shirt over his head.

I could just keep watching him. If we were together, really together and not just...doing whatever this is while I'm not allowed to leave this house, then this is what it could be like in the mornings. He'd get ready to go, I'd watch him, and then go back to sleep. Or get started with my own day. I don't know, exactly.

But I can't keep watching him. He's being quiet on purpose, which probably means he's ready to tiptoe out of here without saying a word to me. I can't be left alone again. I can't let that happen.

"Declan?"

Slowly, he turns to look back at me. I could've sworn he slept next to me last night, but he has shadows under his eyes that make it look like he hasn't slept at all. He lets out a breath when he sees me sitting up.

He licks his lower lip before telling me, "I have to go somewhere."

I push my hair back from my face and take a deep breath. I slept last night. Really slept. Straight through, like nothing in the world could get to me. I blink at the light coming through the curtains. "What time is it?"

"Early. I didn't mean to wake you." Declan puts on his watch and the metal clinks as he says, "About five. I—" He shakes his head. "I must've passed out last night when I got in, otherwise I'd have been ready by now."

"You're leaving?" The realization that I'm going to be alone again hits hard. Nearly a panic. I feel just the way I did last night when Carter brought me up here and left me. The peace I felt while sleeping vanishes.

I don't want to be stuck here. I don't want to be *trapped* here. It doesn't seem like I have options. If I can't leave the house, if I can't call anyone, then that's it. I have to wait until Declan and his brothers tell me what's going to happen. My life is completely in their hands.

Not just Declan's. All the Cross brothers.

The thought of it sends a chill down my spine.

"I have to go," he says softly, like he doesn't want to leave me here, either.

My eyes beg him, but his returning look is one that is apologetic, yet unmoving. Swallowing thickly, I ask, "Are you going to be gone long?"

Declan frowns, tension in his eyes. Something bubbles under the surface, and once again I can't help but notice that he knows much more than I do. It's something that scares me.

"Declan. What's wrong?" I manage to question, not knowing where the line is with us anymore.

"Nothing."

The sheets rustle as I sit up straighter. "Please don't lie to me."

He buttons his crisp white collared shirt, taking his time with each one, but he pauses and looks at me. This time, there's a crackle, almost like electricity in the air. It makes me feel short of breath. The expression on Declan's face tells me that he's making a decision and that I need to understand.

"Declan…" His name is cautious on my lips.

"I want you to marry me."

The world stops. It just seems to hang there, not spinning, no time passing. I'm not even sure my heart is beating. *Marry him? After everything?* I don't know what I imagined he would say, but I didn't see this coming at all.

The shocked word leaves me, "What?" He can't have said what I heard.

Declan's expression is so unnervingly serious that it reminds me of how he was when he came into the bedroom last night. "Don't say yes or no right now."

I can't say anything. I don't say a word. *He asked me to marry him. Declan Cross just said those words to me.*

"I'm going to go out for a while. Then I'll be back, and we can talk. Just don't say no."

My body is ringing. This is all too much, too fast. I can barely breathe.

I'm overwhelmed. I thought the night of sleep had mostly made up for how stressed and tired I was, but it doesn't seem to have done enough now.

Even if I could speak, what am I supposed to say to him? I don't know Declan as well as I thought I did, but I don't think he's lying about having to head out for a while.

I open my mouth to tell him that I won't say no, not right now, and end up nodding instead.

He drops his hands away from the buttons of his shirt. "Can you just let me love you right now?"

All the turmoil in my heart doesn't make me want to deny him. I'm not sure of anything right now, but those words out of Declan's mouth feel like a life raft. Like they're the only things that can keep me from drowning. They feel like something to hold on to, at least to get me through to when he comes back—

I clear my throat just to get a whisper out. "Yes."

He lets out a relieved noise then crosses the room to me, takes my face in his hands, and kisses me into the pillows. Deep and needy like the night before. He's already showered, and the clean scent of him overwhelms me again. His touch, his desperation…it's fucking everything. Nothing else matters.

I can't help that I love him. That when he kisses me, he soothes every pain and worry. I can't help the way my body wants to be near his. I touch his shoulders and his arms and his neck. I pull him in as close as I can. Declan does the same to me. If he didn't have to leave, I think he'd get back into the bed with me and stay here.

Nothing can be simple, can it? There's always something waiting to screw things up.

His mouth on mine doesn't feel screwed up, though I know parts of it are. We still need to talk through everything that happened and why he lied. That seems less important than why he wants to marry me. Uncertainty makes my stomach clench.

"You really want to marry me?" I whisper as he pulls away.

The Cross brothers are strong and powerful, but right now, Declan is doing this for me. He wouldn't do this for anything else. All the emotions of the past forty-eight hours run across his face again. So much fear that echoes my own.

"I need you to." It's strange to hear so much vulnerability from him.

Declan and his brothers don't seem like they would need anything. They're the kind of men who can take it for themselves. But Declan needs this from me. "I need to know you still love me and that you'll be here tomorrow. I need you to know how badly I need you, and want you, and how committed I am to you."

He starts to sit up straighter and I know he's leaving. But I also know I won't be okay until we address what happened. I can't just leave it be. It'll fester and I can't have those thoughts coming back.

He said he had to go, but I can't stop the sentence from rising to my lips. "What happened in that hotel room—"

"Braelynn, I was never going to hurt you." Declan closes his eyes, just for a second, and when he opens them again, the depths of his pain reach the darkness in his eyes. "I could never hurt you, let alone kill you, or let anyone else touch you."

It's a promise I've wanted for most of my life. Tears well up in my eyes, though I know it's not fair to him. He has to leave. I blink them away so he doesn't have to go wherever he's going with this image of me in his mind. "Declan, I—"

"Just think about it, all right? Think about being my wife." His fingers splay through my hair. "I love you."

My heart races as it occurs to me that he truly loves me. This man, I think he really loves me. Declan presses one more kiss to my lips, then pushes off the bed and walks out of the room. He's gone before I can say another word.

"I love you, too," I whisper. He can't hear it, but it feels more honest than to not say it back at all.

Chapter 8

Declan

Apparently the dumb fuck cops work for a detective named Harold Mauer. Mr. Mauer is going to wish I never discovered that information from a cop at the station who works for me.

The scent of cigarettes is pungent. It reminds me of my father if I'm honest. The stack of discarded papers rustles as I step on them. It's impossible to avoid now that the office is trashed. The floorboards creak above me, and I know Carter is still looking for anything and everything that may be hiding in the cop's home.

The alarm is only disabled for another ten minutes but we won't need it. We got what we came here for. What we spent all day planning.

I stare down at what I've found, praying it will end all of this. For Braelynn's sake, I need it to end. Violently and swiftly if I have my way.

Carter's boots appear and then his body is slowly revealed as he climbs down the stairs from the attic. Its access is in the office so it was worth a look.

He's head to toe in black, jeans and a sweatshirt, just like the two of us. The moment I see his hands are empty, a feeling of hopelessness washes over me.

Even though my own hands are occupied.

"He's still tailing them," Jase says while looking at his phone.

Daniel is tailing our detective...who is tailing decoys. Tonight is certainly eventful.

"He just messaged?" Carter asks and Jase nods.

"Do you think Mauer will approach them?" I ask him even though I know Jase can't know for sure. None of us can. This plan is risky in a number of ways.

The detective, who left his house unattended in order to tail the man he believes is me, hasn't stopped sitting on our house since Braelynn got home. We had to get him away and while doing so, provide an alibi.

So one of our men and his girl, who happen to be wearing our clothes and resemble Braelynn and me, are doing us a favor right now and picking up a duplicate marriage license. Of course our lawyer is with them, accompanying the couple as Detective Mauer would imagine he'd do. I'm sure the detective is fucking fuming as he sits in the front seat of his SUV, watching a couple he couldn't crack get married to prevent questions about each other. His cops can't approach her since the files have been drawn against them, so he's forced to do the dirty work.

It was Carter's idea. Distract the detective and keep him away while we pilfer through his place.

It will only work if the detective doesn't approach them. If he does, he'll know it's a setup. Our alibi will be non-existent. Tension rolls through my shoulders.

"How much time do we have until they head back?" I question as we walk downstairs, stepping over the broken glass of picture frames thrown off the walls. It didn't take long to look behind every surface, nook, and cranny of this place.

His office is next, naturally.

"Another twenty but we need to get the hell out of here," Jase answers, picking up his pace.

The smell of gas hits us the moment we make it to the first floor. Jase left the empty jugs by the front door and I don't waste any time grabbing one.

"It feels like old times, doesn't it?" he asks with a grin before taking one more look around and shaking out the last jug.

"It does," Carter agrees, although his eyes never reach ours. He's too busy looking over every inch in the last few moments we have.

Back in the beginning, when everything went to shit and Carter stood up for us, protected and fought for us, and we followed him into this life, it was only us.

For years it was just the four of us. No one knew a single move we made. We didn't rely on a damn soul to get to the top. We fucking earned it.

My grip tightens and I nod, a hint of nostalgia easing some of the concerns.

"Good ol' days," I comment, remembering how different those times were.

There have been more than a few times in the past where we've had to bring the plans in. Shut out some people and limit who we trusted with our plans. It's been years though since it's only been us. Just the brothers. A grim smile almost pulls my lips up. It doesn't quite reach though as I hold my souvenir from this trip tighter. A notebook, with every little detail the detective has on the case against us. Hopefully, it'll include a name here or there or a hint at who the fucking rat is. Or rats. My heart beats harder and anger simmers. All I want is the name of whoever the hell set up my Braelynn. The name of the person who let her take the fall knowing full damn well we'd have her killed.

"He'll know it was us," Carter comments, interrupting my thoughts. Thank fuck.

I clear my throat and look down to the floor, nudging a chunk of ceramic from a broken vase as my brothers talk.

"No shit," Jase answers and then adds, "he won't be able to prove it though."

I take another look around the house that doesn't look like it has been updated since the '80s. This small town on the outskirts of the city is old, way off the highway. So it wasn't surprising to see dated wallpaper in the cramped space and cigarette smoke clinging to the worn leather sofa. It was decently maintained for a single man like Mauer. I imagined he barely spent any time in this place until we got to his office upstairs.

It was a mess before we got there, with ashtrays and empty bottles scattered among filing boxes, but it's trashed now.

And the photos of us from some PI are covered in gasoline...well all apart from the ones tucked away in this little notebook with handwritten details of our whereabouts and businesses. Within the first few pages were hypothetical dealings he suggested we were involved in.

And he's right.

Which means tonight the house will turn to ash and he'll meet that fate soon as well.

Better him than us.

At that thought, Carter opens the door and chilled but fresh air meets us. Jase is behind us and the window he opens creaks before he follows us out.

Even though the podunk town the detective lives in doesn't have a house in sight, we still keep our faces covered as Carter and I climb into the unmarked van.

It's a fair bit away and all the while my mind races. This isn't tit for tat. This isn't skirting around the law and lining pockets. This is war with only one side living at the end.

In my periphery, an orange light brightens and catches my attention.

Jase lights a firecracker and tosses it through the open window in what was once Mauer's living room before running to the open door of the van.

He slides it shut as Carter pulls the car away. The door thuds, the gravel crunches beneath the tires and in the rearview mirror, the fire lights up the window, the flame immediately tall and bright.

Before I can exhale, the house explodes with fire.

CHAPTER 9

BRAELYNN

Emotions are bullshit. I wish I couldn't feel them. Especially when I'm alone.

I almost want to lie down and hide in the covers for the rest of the day, but that won't solve anything. With Declan gone, there's not much more I can learn. That doesn't mean I have to sit here feeling like shit for hours.

I can face the day and feel like shit, too. It's not the first time I've had to and I remind myself that I've certainly felt lower. Progress is a silver lining I suppose.

I get up and make the bed. It's small, but it's something I can actually accomplish. I take my time with it since I don't know when Declan will be back.

Then I go into the bathroom. No need to rush this part,

either. I take a shower, letting the hot water run over my muscles. I don't think I'm sore from my short stint in the interrogation room at the jail. I don't think it was the sex, either. I think it's stress, which is the worst kind of soreness. The hot spray washes away the filth and every negative thought.

I work at it anyway. I get dressed and let my hair dry while I scroll through my phone. Careful not to comment on a single thing. I only watch for entertainment although I hardly feel a thing. It's more of a distraction and with it, I scroll and scroll, thankful that my mind is not left to my own thoughts. That's how I end up spending most of the day. It's easy enough to click from one thing to the next. All the while, I listen for Declan. I'm all too aware that I'm simply biding my time until he comes back and the time is ticking by slowly.

The phone can't keep my attention forever. Nervousness builds in my stomach as I approach the bedroom door. I'm afraid I'll turn the handle and it'll be locked, though I know it won't be. He wouldn't do that to me.

I count to three in my head. On three, I turn the doorknob and throw the door open.

The hallway outside is empty. There's no guard waiting for me when I get to the end of it and open the door to the foyer. None of Declan's brothers are waiting there.

There's nothing but emptiness.

I wish he'd given me some idea of how long this was going

to take. Then again, if he had, I'd be counting the minutes and worrying more if he was late.

My stomach growls loudly. I've been ignoring my hunger most of the day. That was a mistake. Now I'm starving *and* worried *and* emotional over what Declan said this morning. I force my feet to move and take me to the kitchen.

I stride into the kitchen with my head held high, remembering that he said he loves me. If any of his family is there, I hope I look more confident than I feel. I know I don't really belong here. Everything is too uncertain. It would only set me up for failure if I got used to being here, and thought of this as...

Well, anything. It's not my home. This place belongs to Declan and his brothers. To hear Declan tell it, he wants me to belong to him. That sends my thoughts right back to the memory of him getting dressed this morning and the look in his eyes when he spoke to me.

"I want you to marry me." That one statement is the only thing I'm holding onto right now.

The saddest part of it is that I don't know if he really meant it. He looked like he did. He sounded like he did. But he's kept things from me before and lied to me before.

Hell, for all I know, it could be another test. There must be more to it. I don't know what to think of any of this, really, and I can't turn off the worries. I wish I could be one of those people who just puts things out of their mind. I open the refrigerator and feel a cool breeze in my face. There are a few things inside, like leftover takeout and a pasta dish in Tupperware, but none of it looks appealing at the moment. Honestly, I don't know how I could possibly eat, just that I have to because my stomach hurts.

Mostly I just feel empty inside. It's not a good way to approach making something to eat. There's not enough food in the world to fill that space, so it feels a little pointless to go through the trouble of cooking, or even microwaving, anything.

God. Something has to change, and soon, because this isn't any way to live. I have come around to the idea that escaping life forever was probably not the best plan, but what am I supposed to live for now? Nobody can look forward to staying a prisoner. Not having enough information to make choices is enough to drive anybody out of their mind.

"Food," I say to the fridge. "Focus on food."

"You should come hang out with us." The voice behind me startles me so much that I jump. I whip around, the handle on the refrigerator door gripped in my palm. Aria stands there in a baggy burgundy chenille sweater and skinny blue jeans. Her perfectly polished toes are black. Without an ounce of makeup on, she's still stunning. Then there's me in Declan's pajama pants rolled up and a tee shirt I refuse to take off because it smells like him.

We couldn't be more different.

I put a hand over my racing heart and take a deep breath.

Her cherry lips perk up as if it's funny. "So do you want to?"

I don't know what she's talking about. "What do you mean?" Even though she's casual and friendly even, Aria Cross scares the hell out of me. Just like Carter. She is his wife after all.

Aria shrugs. "When they leave, it can give me an anxious feeling sometimes." She reaches across me and opens the fridge.

"They?" I turn her words over in my head. "They left together? Carter and Declan?"

"All of them," Aria answers me. I blink, surprised, and Aria smiles gently at me. "Don't worry, Braelynn. We're safe here. There are guards and nothing to worry about, but I think you'd like it better if you stayed with us."

She purses her lips, shutting the door and apparently coming to the same conclusion I did. "Did he tell you what they're going to do?"

"No."

She hesitates only a moment before asking, "Do you want to know?"

"I..." She has a genuine look on her face, like she might tell me if I said yes. "I don't know. I seriously don't." I don't know why I feel so disappointed in myself. I've never wanted to know. I never wanted to be in this life. All I wanted was him. And look where it's gotten me.

Aria nods, understanding as I swallow down my thoughts.

"Do you want to drink?"

"Yes. Yes, I do." She passes by me grabbing a bag of fruit and nut mix, and I blurt out what I'm thinking before I can stop myself. "He lied to me."

This time it's shame that passes through me.

She pauses, thinking, and looks me in the eye, her gaze a mix of understanding but also one of pity. "This world is fucked up, and so are our men."

"I don't know how to think straight if he's lying to me. Or why I would want to know anything if I won't even know if it's true."

"Given the state he's been in, I doubt he'll ever lie to you again." She nudges me gently out of the way, opens the fridge, and reaches in for an open bottle of wine. She pours us glasses while telling me I should tell Declan how much it hurts. She says he's a lost puppy. It's hard to imagine Declan Cross like that. It's even harder to imagine he'd listen to me. She hands one glass to me, closes the fridge with her hip, and takes a long sip from hers. The chilled glass in my hand is tempting. "Come on. Carter told me it'll be a little bit before they're back. I have something I want to show you."

She doesn't wait for me to agree before turning her back.

I follow her through to the wing of the house where Carter and Aria live. It's warmer than I imagined it would be. The walls are a soft cream but colorful paintings line the way. Giggles reach me through the hall. Children playing, somewhere in the house. I pause when I hear them and it's Aria's short laugh that brings my attention back to her. Aria smiles but doesn't look for them.

"Addison's with them. They're supposed to be in bed, but she spoils them so I'm pretending not to hear it for now."

I forgot there were children here. It's a wonder how they keep their kids separate from all of this. No one ever mentions them. It's as if they don't exist in the real world.

She walks gracefully through the long hallway. All the doors are painted a dark navy blue and complement the gray slate herringbone floor. Where Declan's wing is stark and cold, this wing is lived in. Every detail of this place is beautiful. I'm intimidated by how big this place is, but Aria belongs here. It's hers. Aria's beautiful, and she commands authority. I can't imagine this woman ever being afraid. Even if everything turns out all right between Declan and me, can I ever belong here? I could never be a woman like her. I still can't imagine myself in the world I know to be run by the Cross brothers.

I almost ask her how she does it. How she shuts out some parts and hides others. Instead, she gestures to me to continue, passing the open threshold that leads to her children and other closed doors.

She takes another sip of her wine. "There's a therapist I've seen," Aria mentions casually. "Carter mentioned you may want her info." My cheeks burn. Aria turns to look at me. "Don't worry about it either way. It's good to have her info just in case you decide you want to talk one night. She comes here, so it's all in person, and she can be here in minutes. Actually, she's a lawyer for us, so you're fine to tell her whatever you'd like."

"I'll keep that in mind. Thank you."

Aria stops beside a door, takes a skeleton key out of her pocket, and unlocks it. All the while my heart races and I wonder what Aria knows. I imagine everything.

She smiles at me while she opens the door and I'm blown away at what's inside it. Inside is an art studio, the thick dove gray curtains are drawn over the window. So it's dark and a little intense, and...I like it. There's an energy that radiates in the room.

"Do you like it?" Aria questions as if my opinion matters. I step into the room completely in awe. "I love it," I answer her honestly. Art and canvases take up a lot of the space on one side. They're mostly charcoal pieces featuring abstract adult figures, but there are also acrylic pieces with bright colors and watercolors that feature scenery and children. I can only imagine they're her children. Apart from the art, there's a long dark wooden table that's littered with glass jars filled with brushes and cans of paint. It's a very organized chaos. I can tell each part of it has meaning to Aria. It's where it should be, even if it appears to be a mess.

Turning though, there's another story to tell.

The other side of the studio is similar, but it contains

completely different things. A slim shelf holds several decks of tarot cards. Colorful crystals glint on another shelf. There are glass bottles and candles everywhere. It feels much warmer than the art side, and I'm drawn to it.

There's another long table parallel to the art station, but this one is a warm wood, lower with dainty chairs in gray velvet on either side and a matching sofa that's tufted.

"I could read your cards," Aria suggests as she lights a candle at the center of the table. She moves around the space, putting down her wine glass and picking up a silver tray. An expression of concentration crosses her face as she gathers candlesticks and some kind of oil from one of the shelves.

Just then, the door closes behind us, once again startling the hell out of me.

"Addison, have you met Braelynn?" Aria asks a bright-eyed younger version of herself. There's a softer look about her face, though, and she's a bit more petite.

"Now I have," she comments and offers a beautiful smile. "It's nice to meet the woman Daniel's been telling me about." My eyes widen slightly and she adds, "I'm Daniel's wife," as if that's the part I couldn't put together. And not that I'm concerned about what she's been told. I'm curious how she met Daniel, but I don't want to ask. What if the story is so different from mine that it only adds to this nervous feeling that won't let me go?

Her dark hair falls in gorgeous waves as she comes in and

takes the seat on the end easily. "Are you doing a reading? I want to read, too," Addison says, her voice peppy. Reading tarot cards...my mother never liked tarot cards. I have a feeling she wouldn't much like this room at all.

Aria's at another one of her shelves, gathering some rocks for the tray. "Do you like crystals?" she asks.

I'm not sure if she's talking to me or Addison for a moment. Then I realize they're both waiting for my answer. All eyes on me.

"I do," I tell them both. That's the truth, anyway. "Crystals are very pretty."

The one thing I remember about my great-grandmother were all her minerals and gemstones. She had shelves of rocks, more than Aria that's for sure. When she passed, I was only left one. A dark blue one that I lost at some point in middle school. I keep my story to myself although I nearly tell them.

"I have these for you."

Aria crosses to me and puts one of the stones in my palm. It's smallish and a smooth oval shape with rich earth colors and a hint of blue flash to it. "This one is a *que sera*," she tells me. She goes back to one of the shelves on the wall and opens a drawer beneath it. Aria takes out another stone, then brings it to me.

"And this one is called an Irish Hag Stone, don't mind the name...it works. They help you live soundly and sleep soundly."

"An Irish Hag Stone..." It's a gray rock with a whole in

it. "To help me sleep?" I question. I wish I could keep the skepticism out of my voice, but I can't. It's just a river rock.

"I do have something stronger." Aria doesn't sound offended. "We call it sweets, and it's not a rock...but its side effects might not be good for you right now."

I swallow hard. Aria's talking about my mental state, and she's just used the name of an old street drug.

Addison leans closer to me and gestures for me to take a seat. "Even if it's all in your head, it's in your head, and that's what matters sometimes," she says, her tone gentle.

"We've all been through hard times, Braelynn."

Aria positions the tray near her elbow, picks up a deck of tarot cards, and shuffles them. She holds eye contact with me as her hands move. "I need you to know we're here for you. Whether it's wine and venting or a distraction"—she holds up the cards—"or anything else."

"We've been through it," Addison says, nodding along. "You should know you have us."

"I might not be Carter Cross, but I am a Cross." Addison nods to that, too. "And I want you here."

I almost ask her why—why do you want me here? But I bite my tongue.

Aria smirks as if she can read my mind. "You don't have to ask me. You can ask the cards."

Chapter 10

Declan

Almost 1:00 a.m. and I haven't been home.

We came straight to the club even though it's the last place I want to be. Someone here is a fucking rat. I know it. Hell, it could be every fucking one of them.

The private back room is dimly lit, cigar fog billows from the bar, pool balls smack together, and chatter fills the space.

I've never felt this hollow, never felt this numb to the growing rage. As I lift the beer to my lips, all I can think is that I wish I were home with Braelynn.

"It's important that we stay," Carter murmurs to me. No longer in all black, he wears his typical suit. Daniel and Jase are down in the basement; we told the men we've been there all day and the two of them are wrapping up details of a new deal with a notorious business partner, dubbed N.

As far as they all know, we've been here since nearly 6:00 a.m. "When the news breaks," Carter tells me as if I need reminding, "we need eyes on us here."

"I know," I tell him easily and lean back in my seat in the corner booth.

Carter's curt nod is followed by a gesture to the bartender, Mia. She's been working all night and the only one here not in the business with us. She knows the deal though. Not that it matters. Tonight I don't trust a damn soul but my brothers and maybe a few of these guys I've known all my life.

It doesn't stop the thoughts from racing though. Someone in here, who I've trusted, is a fucking rat.

"Any update from the lawyer?" Jeffery asks, sliding a chair over. Nicholas is behind him. "I let him know the cops are fucking harassing us."

"They got no right coming in here like they are," Nicholas adds. The two are security, broad chested, tall, and nothing but muscle.

"We'll be able to give you a heads up the next time they're on their way," Carter answers and I simply watch for their reaction. Every little detail. Every muscle twitch.

"It's been nonstop, especially that fucker McKinley." They're mostly relaxed given the context, but Nicholas has peeled back the label on his beer bottle.

My men are rattled. Cops come and go; we've dealt with

this shit before. But for Ronnie and Hale to be dead only weeks ago and now with the reputation of rats, tensions are running high.

I'm sure they're all thinking the same things: *What if they told the cops about me? What if the cops are going to get me next?*

"How are you going to know they're coming?" Nicholas questions, his brow pinched.

Strike fucking one Nicholas. Everyone knows you don't ask questions. Surely not from the fucking boss. Jeffery arches his neck to look back at his friend, clearly taken aback that he would ask.

"Not your concern," Nate comes up from behind and gives a smug grin. "You don't have anything to worry about," he tells them easily, although Nicholas's expression morphs to one of realization. "Sorry, boss. Of course," he says and is quick to scurry off after bowing his head. Jeffery follows, thanking us for our time.

"May I?" Nate asks, gesturing to the seat across from us and Carter nods.

I don't miss how Jeffery elbows his friend and the stress clearly written on Nicholas's face. Every moment that passes with this bullshit hanging over our heads is one step closer to chaos and collapse. The two share a shot and the moment passes.

"The judge who signed off on the subpoena to be deposed," Nate questions as he takes his seat. "What are we going to do with him?"

Nate fixes everything. He's solid and stable. Although he's also an asshole and a prick more often than not. What he does, he does well, and that is to take care of problems often without question. Of everyone here, he knows the most. And he knows shit that has never been leaked.

Just then my phone pings and Carter's does as well.

Nervousness pricks through me as I read the caption of the article. I smirk, not letting on, and answer for Carter, "You going to take care of him like you did the cop?"

"Like who?" Nate questions, his lips turning down. I pass him my phone with the breaking news still on my screen. Carter calls out to Mia and she changes the TV station. The screen is quickly filled with video of the aftermath and a woman in a blue blouse covering the breaking news.

"Oh shit," I watch his reaction as he grins at the news. My attention turns to the other men, waiting for one of them to give themselves away. As if it would be that easy.

Nate scratches the back of his head, pulling his jacket up and the motion catches my attention. "I mean if that's what you want for the judge…I think he should be in the house when it happens? Right? And just to make sure you know, that wasn't me. I wouldn't do anything without the green light," Nate says.

Carter chuckles and I take a swig, barely swallowing before Nicholas comments once again. "They're going to come in asking questions about that aren't they?" *Strike two.*

"We didn't have anything to do with it, so they can ask until they turn fucking blue in the face. Don't give them anything." Nate says all the right words. With a nonchalance that brings ease to most of the men.

"You all have the lawyer's number, don't say anything. They don't have anything and we don't have anything to give em'," I add. Carter's quiet, and Jase and Daniel enter but stay on the other side of the bar. Taking in the scene, looking for someone who sticks out from the crowd of our closest men.

"Well they have fucking rats," Nicholas, who nearly slurs his words, bites out, and the bar goes quiet. Chills run down my spine.

"Who's that?" I press, anger brimming, the back of my neck heating. I swear to God if he says her name…Carter's hand finds my shoulder and he grips it, keeping me grounded.

"Scarlet. Hale. Ronnie. We don't know what they told the cops, do we?" Nicholas says like it's obvious and Jeffery tells him to shut the fuck up.

The men around them shift uncomfortably.

"We do. We know everything they told them and they don't have shit," Jase tells the men and orders a shot of whiskey. Letting it blow over even though my entire body is fucking tense, every muscle wound tight.

Scarlet. Hale. Ronnie. Not my Braelynn.

Nicholas seems to catch on to his fuckup and raises his

hands. "I apologize."

"That's why they're pushing so hard and playing their fucking games," I tell him. Fucking thankful he didn't say her name. Grateful he didn't lump her with them. "They're hoping one of you will crack and turn too. We know you guys won't. You've been with us for decades now, haven't you?"

"Yeah," Jeffery says quickly, nodding and swallowing so damn hard I can see his Adam's apple move from here.

"And you"—I stare directly at Nicholas in the quiet bar— "twelve years now, right?"

"Yeah, Boss," he answers. Worry lines around his eyes.

"How's your dad?" I ask him, remembering a while back he was in the hospital.

"He's doing good. Holding up," he answers.

He nods and the bar remains silent.

"Good. Good." I nod and murmur, debating on whether or not to kill this sloppy mother fucker. We've already had too much loss on our side. Morale is low after suffering loss, like the two men I killed for her, and arrests and warrants from cops who are desperate for us to react. The other side needs to take a hit, the other side needs to have loss. And my brothers and I can take care of that ourselves.

"If any of you hears anything, let us know. Don't give the pricks anything other than the lawyer's name. N is waiting for us to be out of this shit before the next deal," Jase says.

"In the meantime, we're taking care of the stress it's

putting on your families," Carter adds.

Jase wraps it up, "If you need anything, call the lawyer and we'll take care of it." He raises his shot glass and adds, "Besides, tonight is a night to celebrate. I love seeing the pricks on the other side get lit up."

"No one is going to jail. We've got it taken care of. Come to work, have a drink, and bide your time," I call out to Mia, grinning. "Let's have a round for the boys. I'm feeling like celebrating tonight after that breaking news."

They all chuckle and order rounds, the atmosphere changes instantly. But inside, everything is raging, every bit of me on edge. And for the next hour I watch everything Nicholas does...and Jeffery too.

CHAPTER 11

BRAELYNN

The truth that nobody can deny is that wine makes things better.

I intended on keeping a distance in Aria's studio, but once the wine hit, I couldn't help myself. I'm no longer watching what I say. No longer holding it together. With a little wine, it's easier to just let go.

They're kind and open. Compassionate and understanding in ways I didn't expect.

They want me here and told me so multiple times, though I'm not sure why. Even with the wine, I don't feel brave enough to question them about it.

Time passes quickly enough and Addison brings enough snacks that they turn into dinner. The three of us share a charcuterie board and another bottle. I'm grateful for the swirls of meat and cheese but more so for the conversation that's so seemingly normal, and the two of them joking about life in general. Everything is so easy that by the time we're digging into the charcuterie board, I'm almost drunk.

I keep a handle on it, though. At least I think I do.

Aria was right. It is better on this side of the house, where there's somebody to talk to. I didn't realize just how anxious I felt with Declan being gone until I let the time pass around me and stopped thinking so hard about it. I wonder how often Aria has had to deal with this kind of thing. I guess it must be often enough that she knows to head to her studio with some wine and a friend and wait it out.

The night is dark, but there's plenty of laughter to be shared in Aria's studio. It's the safest I've felt since all of this began.

Finally, Addison drops her head into her hands, laughing. "I'm going to fall asleep at the table."

"That's it, then." Aria stands up, a warm smile on her face. She rubs at Addison's back. "On your feet, babe. It's time to head to bed."

She leads us out of the studio and locks the door behind her. Then Aria hugs me and Addison. "Braelynn, if you need anything, you text us. We're only a minute away."

"I don't have your numbers," I say into the crush of the hug.

Aria pulls away, laughing, and we exchange phone

numbers. My phone doesn't feel pointless anymore. These two women are people I actually could call if I needed anything. I don't have to worry about hiding from them. There's probably nothing I could say that they would find shocking. The relief is undeniable. So is my gratitude as Aria walks me back to Declan's wing.

"Get some sleep," she says. "They'll be back sooner or later, and it won't help you to stay up worrying."

"I will," I promise her. I'm sure the wine will help me sleep tonight. "Thanks for tonight," I add quietly.

"It'll all be okay," she promises with a gentle smile.

Her compassion was unexpected and I didn't realize how much I needed it.

I didn't believe her earlier in the evening, but now…I think I do. If she and Addison have made it through harder things, like they said, then eventually I'll be on the other side, too.

On my own again, I brush my teeth and wash my face. Clothes discarded, I pull one of Declan's T-shirts over my head. My mind hums with a gentle peace and I even catch myself smiling. I've almost always been kind of a loner and the last friend I really had was Scarlet. What's that say about my friend choices?

This is different though. I can feel that in my bones.

I'm only a step away from climbing into the bed and following Aria's instructions when the bedroom door opens.

I whirl around, feeling in that moment exactly how tipsy

I am. The heat of the alcohol in my blood softens the shock of seeing Declan shirtless. All his muscles are on display, and I have to force myself not to dwell on how hot Declan Cross is. That's not my fault, though. It's just an instinct to notice. Still, worry manages to push through the wine haze.

"What happened to your shirt?"

He scrubs his hands over his face, hesitating for a moment. "It had blood on it." Before, I would have stayed in the bed and let him come to me. This time, I go to him. His eyes flicker and his brow cocks as I put my hands over his chest to feel his heart. It beats strongly under his carved chest. His skin is hot on mine as I balance myself.

He questions, "Are you okay?"

"I'm much better now." I'm reminded of everything that worried me before he left. "You okay?"

He murmurs an answer, "I'm a bit better, I think."

With one hand over mine, he pushes my palm tighter to his chest, then leans forward and kisses my forehead. He smirks a deadly sinful smirk that the devil himself must've taught him and whispers at the shell of my ear, "Give me a second to wash up and I'll make you much better. How about that?"

With goosebumps flowing down my spine, he steps away. A few seconds later the shower runs, and I pad after him into the bathroom.

I don't want to be alone. I don't want the liquid courage to leave me. He's stepping into the shower when his eyes lift and he sees me at the door. Declan raises his arms and pushes the water through his hair, his eyes on mine. Despite all that's happened, I still feel the heat behind that look.

My heart hammers and I'm only vaguely aware of what I'm doing. I want it to be easy again. I want to go back to when it started. That's all I can think about in this moment.

Take me back to that place where I fell in love with him.

I pull his T-shirt over my head and drop it to the floor. Declan's eyes track down my body and follow my hands as I find the waistband of my panties and take them off. My heart in my throat, I cross to the shower and get in with him.

The hot water is soothing and the white noise that surrounds us only urges me to keep going.

At first, I just put my hands to his back, skimming my palms over his shoulder blades. He lets out a low noise and turns, pulling me tight against him. Water slicks between us. Declan tips my face to his and kisses me.

His lips meet mine and I can't help but groan from the simple pleasure in it all.

There's something in his kiss that will always attract me no matter what I do. I could try to run away and never think of him again, but it would be impossible. I'd always imagine the way his tongue slides over mine. He's commanding and possessive, and he doesn't change. The stress of the past couple of days hasn't diminished anything about him. It feels good to let him take control.

My mind hesitates, but only for a second. My body knows what's right, too. Sometimes, my body knows before my mind has had a chance to keep up. Deep down, there's a part of me that knows he's right for me.

"Declan."

"Hmm?"

It's clear he doesn't want to stop kissing me, and I don't really want him to stop, either. I let him keep going for another minute until I'm so hot and bothered from his body and from the wine and the way he's kissing me that I push at him a little.

Declan pulls back, water droplets clinging to his eyelashes. "Yeah?"

I dare to do what Aria said. To talk to him and tell him how I'm feeling. "We need to…fix things. Between us."

His brow furrows, and he manages to look solemn, even though we're naked in the shower and the water sprays against his back. A stray droplet hits me in the eyes every so often and makes me blink. It could be the wine giving me this courage, or the time I spent with Aria and Addison, or just the realization that's slowly sinking in.

It takes him a moment of studying my expression before he answers, "Tell me how we can fix it." His voice is soft and patient.

My throat tightens and my heart hammers. I don't want to screw this up.

"I realized...I'm realizing, right now..." Declan's patient with me. His hands slide to my waist and he holds me close to his body, but he doesn't rush me. "I never want to go back to that place we were. I can't handle not being able to trust you. So I need you to understand that I'm not going to respond well to certain things."

He nods but stays quiet, giving me the space to say what I need to say.

"I think I'll be okay if you don't lie to me." This is the part that scares me to admit out loud. People like the Cross brothers are used to having to lie. They move in worlds where lying and violence are part of everyday life. Somewhere from some source of courage, the words tip out with a fierceness I didn't know I had. "No more tests. No more white lies. And no more secrets. They make me feel like I'm going crazy, and I can't do that."

Declan waits until he's sure I'm finished, then leans in and kisses the tip of my nose. It's a sweet, tender gesture and I know he wouldn't do that for me unless he truly had feelings for me. "Promise me you'll marry me, and I'll tell you everything you want to know. That's all you have to say, and I'll protect you from everything in the world, Braelynn. You won't have to be afraid again. I'll never lie to you again."

Marry me. He said it again.

My blood runs hot as his promises sink in. The water continues to crash around us and his hands stay on my hips, my hands on his chest. Our eyes locked.

That's what I want. I want the safety he's offering me. I want him to wrap me in his arms and never let go. But marriage?

"Why would you want to marry me?" I whisper the very real question out loud. I know there has to be another reason.

CHAPTER 12

DECLAN

No matter how much she tells me she's okay, I can see the pain lingering there. The distrust. She's not a good liar. I already knew that though.

"I don't just want you to marry me because I love you and I don't want you to ever doubt it. I need you to marry me to protect you from legal shit."

Her lips part but she stops herself from asking whatever it was that came to her mind.

The hot shower sprays around us and I barely hear the noise. Every thought that has screamed in my head, demanding to be heard, bombards me.

All of them about Braelynn. Every single one that kept me up while I sat against the concrete wall of the cell, every thought as I searched Mauer's home looking for anything that could end this.

It all points to one end. It all brings me back to her.

Taking one step forward, I move her out of the spray, her long dark hair slicked back over her tanned skin. The steam billows around us, keeping us warm as the water hits my back.

When her eyes find mine, it's a trance. I'm lost in her longing gaze.

Her fingertips splay between the short hair on my chest and her gentle touch is everything I need to soothe the pain that hasn't let go.

She reaches up, on her tiptoes, and kisses me. A soft, sweet peck but I need more. I need something I don't know she'll understand. Something raw and real to me, but maybe I'm out of my fucking mind.

"Can I share something with you?"

"You're asking?" she questions playfully, but her eyes read that she's worried. No longer on her tip toes, she takes a half step back and brushes the hair from her face.

I don't know where to start, but I let the thoughts escape and hope it makes sense, "My parents were married Catholic, they were young and it was in an old church with a family priest."

Her brow pinches and she whispers, "okay," as if she's following. I've never felt so nervous in my life.

"She said that wasn't her wedding day though. She told

me stories. She said they were meant to be. That they loved in another time."

I watch her swallow, her chest rising and falling as I admit, "I haven't slept and my mind is racing." Water sprays against my face and I stand up taller, rubbing it out of the way. I'm sure I'm not making sense. "I'm not at my best and I feel like I'm losing my damn mind, but all I can think about is you."

"Declan are you okay?" she questions and the truth is, I'm not. I won't be okay until she's mine in every way.

"No," I admit.

"It's okay," she consoles me and I shake my head.

"It's not."

"I need you," I admit to her, the memory of nights ago coming back again.

"I'm right here," she whispers, her hands once again finding my chest.

The chuckle is genuine as I tell her, "My naive girl, I don't just want you in this world. I need you in the next. I don't think I've ever had a choice. I think we've done this before. It's why when I'm with you, everything is right and the world isn't so dark. In another lifetime, maybe when life wasn't so fucking brutal." I let every thought that's haunted me pour out of me.

"I think I've loved you forever and always will. That I've always belonged to you, and you've always belonged to me. I want to protect you, keep you safe, and make sure you are loved. It's all I want in this world and the next. Put me out of my misery and tell me you'll marry me." I swallow thickly, barely able to breathe, and then close the short distance between us, my forehead nearly touching hers.

"Tell me you'll marry me. If you don't, I won't survive this," I murmur to her. She might not know just how true these words are. Or how vulnerable it is to tell her.

Hell, she might not believe a word of what I've just said when it's the barest of truths and I would never tell another soul about them because I'm all too aware of how it could crush me.

She could destroy the last piece of who I am in this moment and I know it all too well.

"Declan," she murmurs my name with hesitancy as her eyes search mine and something inside of me cracks. I'm desperate to hold it together.

"Don't say anything but yes." My throat tightens and I inch toward her, "Just say yes."

My heart pounds once, then again and again, all the while her dark eyes beseech mine.

Finally, she whispers, "Yes."

Relief is instant as is the need to claim her. Her lips are first and then my hands roam her body.

Mine. She's truly mine.

"I love you," I whisper in between urgent kisses. She presses against my chest, forcing me back just enough to tell me, "I love you too. Even if you scare me."

With her in my arms, I turn her so her back is to my front. The warm water pours at my back and I let it go, not interested in a damn thing other than her. Loving her and taking that fear away.

I enter her fully in one swift stroke and it's fucking heaven. The way her back arches, her breasts press into my hands. The sharp intake of breath and then soft moan that pours from her lips. The way every inch of her heat feels around my cock...heaven. Braelynn is my heaven.

How I'm able to speak is a mystery to me as our eyes meet. Her gaze reflects back everything I've been feeling. "Watch the mirror," I whisper at the shell of her ear and seemingly reluctantly, she moves her gaze to our reflection and I do the same.

With another thrust, her palms smack against the stonewall of the shower. My gaze drops to her peaked nipples and supple breasts as they sway with each thrust.

My heart pounds as the pleasure intensifies with each stroke. With an arm bracing her, holding her close to me, I make love to her. Deeply and fully capturing her lips as she comes undone for me. Grateful that she's here with me still and able to love.

CHAPTER 13

BRAELYNN

I love Declan and he loves me. But Carter also made it clear that this is the way to keep the law from using me to get to Declan.

I never thought a man would one day propose to me by simply saying that he needed me to marry him. I never thought that the marriage would be for reasons other than love. Love has a lot to do with it, of course, but above all, Declan wants to protect me. Somehow, this is the best way to get the law on our side, at least a little.

It wasn't just the wine that said yes last night. My damn heart refused to say no.

"This feels so strange," I whisper to him in front of one of the glass cases in the jewelry store. The jeweler, an older man with a neat gray suit, hovers nearby, pretending to look through a catalog although he keeps glancing up and has asked me several times if I want him to take out a ring to look at. Nate stands outside the shop and I can just barely see his suit in the large bay window.

"It's better this way."

I can't help but look around the store as the nerves flip in my stomach. "The whole store is closed for us, though, you don't think—"

"I think it's safer," Declan says, with a finality to his tone. He's the one who called ahead and had the store closed down. "Don't worry about anyone else. Just focus on choosing a ring. More than one ring, if you want."

My laugh feels too loud for an empty jewelry store. "What would I need more than one ring for?"

"I want to spoil you." He kisses the back of my neck, his lips soft and warm. "If you want two rings, you'll have two rings. I'm sure there are other things you'd like. Choose anything. This day is for you."

The kiss makes me shiver. I love him, but I'm scared. It's moving very quickly and I'm not so naive that the reality hasn't dawned on me.

Once I marry Declan, I'm in this life. I can't imagine they'd ever let me leave. And it's all happened so fast that I have mixed feelings about whether this will work. Declan seems to believe that if we get married, I'll be shielded from having to testify. He thinks it'll save me from the worst of the fallout.

What if it can't, though? What if a shotgun wedding won't change anything?

I haven't even told my mother. Real life as I know it is gone forever the moment I slip this ring on my finger. I know it. Sober, or rather hungover, me apparently has cold feet.

Declan puts his hand on my jaw and turns my face to the side so he can kiss me. With his body behind me and his hand at my waist, my worries are chased away...for the moment. Everything feels like it's going to be all right when he kisses me.

My heart races and my body leans against his.

Declan breaks the kiss, his eyes lingering on mine for a few beats. "Look at the rings," he says softly, and turns my head so I'm looking at the glass case again. "What about that one?"

He points to a pear-shaped diamond with a band of pink diamonds. It's beyond pretty and delicate and looks way too expensive to be on my finger, but I can't take my eyes off it. Declan clears his throat and the jeweler comes around to the case without a word spoken. The keys on his hips jingle unneeded as he unlocked all the cases when we first arrived. He offered us champagne, too, which I declined. I think last night did a bit of a number on me.

As we wait quietly, Declan's hand on the small of my back, the man opens a panel in the back, takes out the ring, and shows it to the both of us, talking about the size of the diamond, the cut, and the artist.

I never knew there were so many ways to judge the worth of a diamond. In my wildest dreams I never thought I'd be shopping at a store like this, picking out a ring with a man like Declan Cross.

The jeweler hands the ring to Declan, who slips it on my finger. He holds my hand in both of his and turns the ring one way, then another, viewing it in the light. His dark eyes meet mine, "What do you think?"

"I love it," I whisper without taking my eyes off his.

"Is it the one?"

I hesitate, my heart racing, and Declan informs the jeweler that he wants to keep looking.

"We'll keep an eye on this one." Declan hands it back to the jeweler, and we continue moving around the cases in the quiet jewelry store. My heart beats faster. I really did love that ring, but maybe I just loved Declan's hands on mine. Maybe I would love any ring like that.

It turns out that no, I don't love any ring like that. We try a few more, moving slowly between the cases. I keep glancing at Declan to see if he's getting impatient with me, but he doesn't.

"Are you upset?" he asks, his voice quiet when I shake my head after another ring. "You look sad," he tells me when I only stare up at him. It's beautiful, it just doesn't make my heart beat faster. "If you don't like any of the rings, we can go to another jewelry store."

I've never seen Declan Cross as nervous as I do today.

"I'm not upset with you and I love these rings. Any number of them would be perfect...I was just thinking about my mom."

"What about her?" he asks although his gaze is on the case. I'm sure he knows exactly what I'm thinking.

"I miss her," I admit. "It feels wrong to get married without her blessing. She'd want to know about this." What I'm about to say isn't fully true, so I rethink the sentence.

"I can understand that." He doesn't offer a solution though and my heart sinks. We move to the next case and instead of swallowing down my thoughts, I blurt them out. Awkward jeweler be damned.

"And...once we're married, I have to go back to some kind of normalcy. It can't always be...you know." I motion toward the empty jewelry store.

Declan cracks a smile and it changes his entire expression. His eyes light up, and he looks softer than he has in a long time. "You can't always be in an empty jewelry store? I don't plan on this being a weekly event."

"You know what I mean. I definitely don't want to hide our marriage from the world."

"I don't plan to hide our marriage. Trust me on that one, Braelynn."

The door opens with a little ping and I turn to see Nate hovering near the front door. Our driver apparently wanted out of the cold for a minute.

"Hey," Declan whispers and gets my attention once again,

his dark eyes peering into mine. "I want you to be happy," he says definitively. "And safe. That's what I want from this. If being happy includes telling your mom, then we should do something about that."

My heart does this little flip every time he makes it easy. Why does it feel like I can let go now. Why does it feel like everything is going to be all right, even though I know I should be scared?

"We can tell her. We can have her over or you can go see her," he says and when he swallows, his Adam's apple draws my eyes down.

"Are you nervous?" I whisper somewhat teasingly and he flashes a charming smile.

"Let's get you a ring," he answers with a blush creeping into his cheeks.

"I want that other ring," I announce. "The one I loved first with the pink diamond band."

Declan smiles and takes my hand gently in his. "Are you sure? You're not saying that because you think I want to be done?"

I stare into his dark eyes and I know I'm still scared and that it isn't possible for me to prepare for what's to come. But if he keeps loving me, I'd follow him straight to hell. I whisper, "I'm sure."

Declan calls the jeweler back over, and we try on that first ring I loved one more time. The older man isn't pushy. He's kind and warm and patient, and as soon as he's sure we don't feel pressured, he moves to the register.

As he's placing it into a black velvet box, I notice the red and blue lights in the reflection of the jewelry cases. Tension grows in my shoulders and I pull on Declan's sleeve. I can't even speak as the lights flash.

It takes Declan a second longer and Nate calling out, "Boss." He wheels around and meets Nate's eyes. Nate looks back at him, his expression set, stoic, and resigned. His eyes are wide though, as if asking what he should do.

Declan takes me toward the door as the cops climb out of the cop car. The car doors slam shut barely being heard over my pounding heart. Another police vehicle pulls up behind them. "I'm sorry my sweet girl," Declan says under his breath. He puts his arm around me and pulls me in tight. I can feel his barely restrained anger in his tone. "I love you."

My heart hammers. "Wait. What's happening?" I question in a single breath even though I already know.

Nate clears his throat to ask Declan and steal his attention from me. "You or me, you think?"

Declan's hand clenches on my waist. "I'm just hoping it's not both." Declan glances at the man behind the counter who says he didn't call anyone.

"Just make sure she gets her ring," he tells him while texting someone.

"Declan what's happening?" I ask him again as the cops

line up beside their cars. No one has made an effort to come in, but they're obviously here for us. "I'm letting my lawyer know," he tells me and then addresses Nate. "I don't want them to come in here."

"All right we'll go out. You ready?"

Declan leans down and kisses me and then tells me, "There's a chance that I'm going to be taken down to the station," he tells me calmly as nervous waves shoot through me. This can't be real.

"I need you to stay here. Nate and I are going to go see what they want and you don't need to worry, just stay here."

My throat dries and I only nod in response. Not wanting to believe it and being struck with reality.

I watch numbly as they both stride out and before the door even closes, a cop says loud enough for me to hear, "Mr. Cross, we have a warrant for your arrest on suspicion of arson."

My heart pounds and my legs feel weak.

The cops converge on Declan. He doesn't look back at me but Nate does. With a nod of his chin, Declan sends Nate back into the store. The bell pings, but I could care less.

My heart is fucking breaking.

There's nothing I can do but witness it. They put him in cuffs and get him into the car, talking the whole time although I can't hear them. I almost feel compelled to do something.

Anything. My feet move past Nate and my hand grips the

door but Nate stops me.

"Declan doesn't want you out there," he tells me and although his words are harsh, his tone is gentle.

I watch them ride away, one after the other, although a cop car in the back stays parked. The officers are watching Nate and me. All the while my head whirls and my heart races.

I'm so shook up that Nate has to put the box in my hand. "Declan's going to want you to have this when he gets out," he tells me and I look up at him to see his brow raised, as if asking me if I understand.

I only swallow and nod. Everything is numbing and surreal.

"We need to get you home," he says, steadily, and then he takes me to the car. I climb into the passenger seat, my hands still shaking. With one hand around the other, I squeeze them tight, the visual of Declan being arrested playing over in my head again and again. Nate looks up and down the street, then gets behind the wheel. He starts the car. I feel him look over at me, but I don't look back.

"Are you all right?"

"I don't know." He drives us away from the jewelry store. It fades away behind us like we were never there.

"It's going to be all right." Nate sounds sure of himself. "They don't have anything."

I haven't forgotten the last time I was alone with Nate. The visual of him killing Scarlet creeps into the back of my mind and I find myself scooting closer to the window.

"Hey, it's going to be okay. You don't have to worry," he tells me again and this time I peer over at him to find him glancing between the road and me. "It's going to be all right," he reassures me again.

I can't help but see Scarlet again and all the events unfolding. It's hard to breathe and I have to close my eyes. It plays out in my mind, beginning to end, as if no time at all has passed.

One breath in and one breath out.

"You want to change the station?" Nate asks after a minute.

All I know is that I can't afford to forget who these men really are. I can't let myself believe that everything really will be okay. I stare down at the black velvet box. This is my life now and I honestly don't know that I have much of a choice about any of that.

"No thank you," I tell Nate. I whisper as I stare out of the window, begging my mind to think of anything else. "The music's fine."

CHAPTER 14

DECLAN

The interrogation room feels almost like a second home now. Hell, they should put my name on the damn door and reserve it for my ass.

The metal door opens and slams shut. I don't bother to lift my gaze from the table; I know exactly who it is who's walked in. His heavy breathing gives it away.

Mauer is a bigger prick than I could have imagined. There's a slight yellow tinge to his teeth that reminds me of my father's friends growing up.

The question that irritates me the most is how the hell did I not know about this fucker?

With reddened cheeks that hang just slightly with his older age, and dark bags under his eyes, Mauer looks like shit.

Sleepless nights and anger coat his expression. He narrows his eyes, "You're not going to get away with it."

Heat licks across my skin as anger threatens to come to the surface. Half of his notes had whereabouts for meetups with our business partner N. Half were about Scarlet and my Braelynn.

Scarlet was his informant but she knew shit she shouldn't have. There are two possibilities:

There's another rat, which is what my gut is telling me.

Someone gave Scarlet information...which could have been my unsuspecting Braelynn.

I swallow thickly as I lean back in the metal chair. The two front feet come off the ground just slightly and I let it fall back down to the ground recklessly.

"Get away with what exactly? Suspicion of arson is what you got me on...which is weak as fuck. Given I have a solid alibi and you just decided it was me—" I lean forward, clasping my hands and giving him a look of pity as I add, "That's not how the law works."

I shouldn't be saying shit, but I'm pissed.

Today was all for my girl. To give her the world and spoil her and make sure she knows she's protected. And then this dumb fuck showed up...rage simmers in my blood.

"Listen here you little shit. I know every fucking move your family has taken. Every associate, every dime that's been funneled and washed, every time you pieces of shit jaywalked," he huffs in a rushed breath to practically sneer, "I only let it go so I could get to the bigger fish."

My lip quirks a twitched smile, I know he's full of shit. There is no bigger fish and both of us know it. We own the whole fucking coast. If he knew everything, he'd sure as fuck know that.

I let my knuckles rap on the table, finding myself falling into Carter's habit. His gaze flinches down to my hand. He's nervous. The detective shows signs of spiraling. Either from having a personal loss, or maybe from losing his book of bullshit on us. Maybe, like the two cops who worked for him, he might be losing the case.

"I really wish I could help you, but I have no fucking clue what you're talking about," I tell him, sitting back in my seat once again.

He rolls his shoulders and the wrinkled suit stretches over his broad frame. Mauer takes a moment to crack his neck and all the while I wait. If his clenched fist is anything to go by, he's going to punch me.

That would be all too easy for me though. A restraining order against him would seal the deal. His gaze meets mine, narrowed and enraged, telling me he's all too aware of that fact.

He's yet to sit. Leaning over the table, knuckles of both fists against the metal, he tells me, "We know the money coming into that bar isn't the money going out."

My heart beats all wrong once and then twice. He's

referring to the info from Braelynn. Or at least information only she was supposed to have. I swallow thickly, trying not to think of that right now.

"All you have are theories and made-up evidence. My lawyer alerted me to those numbers and they don't match what's filed."

He only grunts.

"Your detectives should have done their due diligence, none of that information matches what was filed."

Heat coats my skin as I realize, had I given Braelynn the real numbers, I could be locked up for evasion, fraud, and laundering. More than once in the last decade I've narrowly escaped hard time. Never due to a woman I loved though. Hell...I've never loved a woman. I'm out of my depths.

"Mr. Cross?" his hardened voice raises and I'm brought back to the present. Back to being irritated and wanting nothing more than to get the fuck out of here.

"What?"

"You really think you're going to get away with this?"

"Away with what exactly?"

"With everything you and your brothers have done. It's going to catch up to you sooner or later and you're all going down."

I crack my own neck, more irritated than anything else. "Do you have any actual fucking questions for me?"

"I didn't bring you in to talk," Mauer tells me before

standing up straighter. "You'd plead the fifth in any deposition like you have before. No fucking use."

My brow cocks as I wait for him to tell me whatever the fuck it is he wants to get off his chest.

"You burned my house down to announce war," he tells me, heading to the door. "I brought you in here to inform you that the challenge was accepted."

"Is that right?" I ask him.

And with that he leaves me. My shoulders rise and fall as the anger grows inside me. I keep calm, waiting to be released. All the while, I realize we can find the kink in the chain.

All I need to know is how the fuck I had no idea this prick was watching us. Somewhere along the line one of my men knew and chose not to tell me. If I find that thread and pull, every man who works for me but failed to do their damn job is as good as dead. Starting with every cop on payroll who knew the two who worked for Mauer.

Chapter 15

Braelynn

I know the second I step through the door that I won't be able to sit alone in Declan's bedroom. Lying in bed as the memories of all we've done and all we've been through fight for all my attention. I'll only get trapped in my thoughts and emotions, and that will make me feel even more helpless.

The little black velvet box from the jeweler's sits on the dresser and I stare at it longer than a sane person would. Swallowing thickly, I tell myself that I can at least try to wait patiently. I don't have to call for help every time there's a problem. The part of me that wants to be as independent as I possibly can says I should only reach out if something's really wrong.

That it's good for me to be alone right now.

But the other part of me knows that's very much not the case. There hasn't been much lately that serves as a good memory, other than being with Declan, so it's all left me shaken and unsure of myself.

Without thinking, I move through the motions. I take off my coat and hang it up. Go to the bedroom and wash my face. I pull off my top and replace it with a soft sweater. It's comforting, it's luxurious even, but it doesn't stop the racing thoughts in all this silence.

Then, as slowly as I can, I go back to the shared space of this massive estate and to what seems to be the gathering spot: the kitchen.

All the while my heart beats harder and harder not knowing how any of this will go.

The clock on the oven says it's only been ten minutes. Ten minutes of shaking, ten minutes of triggering moments that threaten to undo the barely put together composure I'm holding onto. I've never been one to reach out for help, but something tells me I need to. I grab my phone and send Aria a quick text. *Are you busy? Can I come hang out?*

I'm in the studio and have a glass of wine with your name on it, she texts back.

It's a huge house and these wings are like mazes, but I remember the way to her studio. Aria opens the door just as I raise my hand to knock.

"Hi." She looks concerned, but not worried, which might

be just what I need at this moment. "You doing okay?" She moves slightly, her black silk maxi dress swaying around her hips as she does. The dress is simple, and she's only brushed her hair, yet everything about her looks expensive in a way that I could never achieve. An easy confident beauty. She ushers me into the room and I'm hit with the scent of roses and lavender. Her candles are lit.

I don't move just yet, trying to smile but my lips barely curve. "Not really. But I guess there's nothing I can do but wait for him to get out. And...I'm hungry." Before I can ask her if she's eaten, she cuts me off.

"That last one we can do something about." She glances behind her and then quickly blows out the candles. "Would you rather cook or order something?"

"Cook," I say instantly. "I need something to do...you know?"

She nods in understanding as she steps out into the hallway. "Cook first, then we could read cards, if you wanted. Or just talk. Or watch a show." She rattles off options and doesn't hesitate to the lead the way. The mix of emotions that comes over me is sudden and unexpected.

This woman owes me nothing. She barely even knows me. Yet she walks beside me, willing to stop whatever she was doing just to be here for me.

My throat tightens as I tell her I'll be better once I've eaten. I think.

"I get that, too." Aria locks up the studio. We head to the kitchen as she tells me Carter is going to fix it all and everything will be all right. All the while she talks. She never stops talking as she rummages through cupboards and the fridge. "Pasta and Bolognese sauce?"

I can only nod, not trusting myself to speak and just grateful that she's doing this.

Aria gets out a pot and passes it to me. It's one of the fancy ones, heavy, and looks brand new. With the tap above the stove, I fill it and then light the burner.

"So...how'd it go? Before...before the cops showed up and killed the mood?" she asks me as she leans against the counter.

It takes me a moment to speak up, I have to clear my throat first.

"It was really good." I turn away from the pot. My mom thought the old saying about watched pots was true, so we always angled ourselves away while we waited for the water to heat. "Until it wasn't."

"Before that, though, you had a good time? Like did you find a ring?" she asks, glancing down at my hand that is very much lacking a diamond.

I nod, and then wish I had it with me. I wish I could show her.

"I bet he loved that." Her tone is soft and comforting and something about it soothes a sadness that won't let go.

"I think he did," I say and a gentle smile finally pulls my

lips up.

"Well whenever you're ready I would love to see it," she tells me while reaching up for a wine glass.

I can't help it, I ask her what I couldn't ask Nate, "Do you know why?"

She shakes her head gently as the glass hits the counter. As she removes the cork from the bottle she says, "I wouldn't worry about it. Carter said the warrant should have never been approved."

"So he knows?" I ask, my tone hopeful and I don't know why.

She pours the wine, humming a yes and then says, "I wouldn't ask unless you really want to know."

I can only nod and then look back to check the water. Since its not boiling, I check the flame and realize it's on low. I increase it, pushing down the emotions and all the questions piling up.

I don't want to know. I don't want to be a part of it. But my heart clenches, I want to know that he'll be all right.

"What else?" she prompts me, changing the subject back to the good parts of today. "Was it tough to pick out a ring?"

"No. Nothing could measure up to the first one I really loved. Took a little while to convince myself of that, though." I can't help where my mind goes, "Maybe if I hadn't taken so long—"

"Hey." Aria looks me in the eyes. "Don't second-guess yourself like that. None of this has anything to do with you."

I only nod and try to avoid her prying gaze for as long as I can until I'm forced to look up.

Aria gives me a look that's only slightly skeptical. "It seems like something else is on your mind."

"I'm scared for Declan."

"Don't be."

She's so confident in her answer, lifting the glass to her lips and offering me one. I let out a laugh. "I don't think I can stop worrying. I was also thinking about my mom and just...being married without her there, or without her even knowing. Getting married is it, you know? It means I'll be in this life forever, and it doesn't make sense to me that she wouldn't know about it." The words pour out of me in exasperation.

There's so much that goes into a life. Kids laughing in a bedroom when they're supposed to be asleep. Cooking meals with your husband, as long as he's not in jail. A thousand little things like a wedding ceremony that your mom can be at and wedding pictures to look back on and....things like a wedding gown.

Aria nods. "Invite her here. Does she like Italian?"

I swallow thickly, knowing the first question my mother is going to ask me. "What about Declan?"

She pats my arm, then turns to put a saucepan on the stove. "He'll be out soon. It's only going to be a deposition or an interrogation. They've all been through this before. Could be a few hours, could be a day or so."

I shake my head slightly and stay silent. I don't like the thought of Declan being questioned or interrogated. I don't want him anywhere but next to me.

The flame clicks on and Aria scoots me to the right so she can take over the cooking.

She talks all the while gathering an onion, fresh tomatoes, garlic, a few cans of crushed tomatoes, and spices. "He means it when he says he'll protect you. Carter will, too. And now that the paperwork is filed and you two are legally married, they can't question you about him." Aria gives me an encouraging smile. "So I wouldn't worry about that, either."

A shiver goes down my spine. It's eerie how Aria knows everything without me telling her. "I actually...still have to sign it."

She whips her head around toward me. "Well, sign it." Aria glances back at the saucepan and the ingredients she's arranged on the countertop. She lifts her hands, but then she pauses and looks back at me. "You *are* going to marry him, right?" Her question is softly spoken, not judgmental, but once again concerned.

"Yes. I want to marry him." I answer without thinking and only after it's spoken do I realize how true it is.

"I love him," I whisper to her but also to me as tears prick the back of my eyes.

Aria lets out a heavy breath. "Okay, good."

She's clearly relieved, but my stomach drops from the

way she said it. I'm beginning to understand the situation with far more clarity than I've had before. If I don't marry Declan, things could go very badly for me. I don't really have a choice, do I?

It makes all those things I wanted to experience with my mom by my side feel less important and more important at the same time. Obviously, not getting to cut a wedding cake with my mom looking on isn't as important as our safety. But knowing that our lives are so fragile that we have to do everything in our power to protect ourselves makes me want it even more.

I want her to know my husband. I want her to know who I am when I'm with him. Who I've grown to be. I'm certainly not the same woman I was months ago, only worried about how I was going to pay my rent. My entire world has changed. I wouldn't be the same without knowing the Cross brothers. And Declan wouldn't be the same without me.

"They might be brutal men," Aria states, breaking into my thoughts. "But they fight and love with the same intensity."

There's a half-smile on Aria's face when she turns back to the saucepan. It makes me think of her with Carter. The two of them as a couple. She's kind and generous, and he's a Cross brother, but...they clearly work. The two of them have overcome whatever fears either of them had. It probably happened over time.

I've heard stories though. I know she grew up in this life

and she has a brutal side to her as well. I wonder if she was always like this or if Carter made her this way.

I wonder what I'll grow to be and how much like her I may become. My heart pangs, even Declan used to be different. This world turned him brutal.

There's a massive difference between how I felt about Declan as a child and when I walked in here weeks ago. How I feel about him now is just as different. Back then, I mostly felt bad for Declan and his brothers. Losing their mom and their father being the way he has...

It's one of the reasons I was so drawn to him. He was like a broken bird. He only needed someone to love him. I could feel it even as a little girl.

So to love him now...of course I do. Of course I love him. It's not him that holds me back, it's this fucked-up brutal world and all that comes with loving a man like him.

My signature on a sheet of paper doesn't seem like as much protection as bodyguards and guns, but it is. It keeps me safe in a way that Declan might not always be able to with brute force and an intimidating presence.

If I can understand that, so can my mom. Somehow, we can make this work. We have to, because life isn't worth living without the people I love.

My face heats up at the thought. It's as if I blinked and I see it all so differently. I was so scared before that I couldn't see how much they meant to me, or how much I meant to them. Everything seemed hopeless. Now I know that it's not, and here I am, tempted to give in to those feelings.

"They care for you, Braelynn." Aria doesn't turn to face me as she stirs the meat sauce in the pan, but her voice is gentle. "I was there when the lawyer called, and he told us—" She shakes her head. With a few taps of the spatula on the edge of the pan, she puts it down and finally looks at me. "I care for you, too. So if you ever feel low again, will you tell me? I'm here for you. We're all here for you."

"Ever feel low?" I whisper the way she said it and feel my throat get tight. We both know what she's talking about. The window incident.

"I don't judge you," she says firmly. "All of us have our issues."

"I think…" I run my hand over my hair. Behind me, the water is starting to bubble. I can hear them popping at the surface. "I think I mostly just don't want to talk about it."

"That's fine." She reassures me with a quick smile. "We don't have to talk about it. We can do whatever you need."

Aria's kind. She's almost too kind, which makes me feel more conflicted. I don't know if I can trust her. I don't know if I can trust anyone. Guilt twists my stomach for even having the thought in the first place.

What the hell is wrong with me? With the water boiling, I shove it all down and grab the box of spaghetti.

The guilt doesn't go away as I put the noodles into the

boiling water and set a timer. Aria works on the sauce, stirring in spices, and we stand side-by-side in front of the stove.

Neither of us says much, and Aria seems fine with not talking. That makes me feel even guiltier. I don't have any business not trusting her, I guess. She hasn't done anything to make me think she'd try to hurt me on purpose.

Hell, I'm the one who messaged her.

I'm hungry and emotional. That's all this is. I can't be expected to think straight when today has gone the way it has and I'm starving.

Aria takes down plates before I can even ask where they are. She prepares the plates while all I do is watch. "Come on. Sit down and let's figure it out."

For a second, I think she's talking about the whole situation, and that doesn't seem like something we can solve over a plate of pasta. "Figure out what?"

She turns to look me in the eye as she answers, "When would be a good time to meet your mom and to introduce her to your new husband."

CHAPTER 16

DECLAN

That fucker didn't let me out of there till 3:00 a.m. I sat in a room doing fuck all with nothing but my damn thoughts and an old-ass heater clicking on and off every twenty fucking minutes.

There are four bottles of whiskey on the bar cart and I choose the one closest. I don't give a fuck which one I drink so long as it'll stop my racing thoughts. I just want to sleep and have a moment of rest.

"You all right?" Carter's voice startles me from behind.

"Nothing I haven't been through before," I answer him. He's dressed in black silk pajama bottoms and looks like he rolled out of bed. "What are you doing up?"

"Waiting for you to get home. Did you check on Braelynn?"

he asks me...which is out of the norm.

"Yeah, before coming out here." She's sleeping soundly, wearing the ring I bought her, although I keep those details to myself. "Why?"

"Paperwork isn't filed yet?" he asks rather than answering my question.

"We'll get it postdated and turned in tomorrow."

"Good."

"Why did you want to know if I'd checked on her?"

"I didn't feel comfortable checking the cameras and Aria was asleep. Wanted to make sure she was all right."

A tinge of something warm flows through my chest. It's quickly extinguished though.

"Any thoughts from the interrogation?"

"Not so much an interrogation as it was a threat."

Carter only grunts a laugh, tilting the whiskey bottles to read each label. "Someone had to know Mauer was poking around and they didn't tell us."

He pauses, his brow raising as he looks from the bottles back to me, "You sure?

Nodding I elaborate, "He has info going back almost a year. There's no way at least one of the cops in our back pocket didn't know. The question is, why didn't they tell us?"

"Someone else is paying them off?" he guesses, and his guess is as good as mine.

"Could be."

"Let's pay a visit to some friends tomorrow and see what we can find." I nod and before I can pour a glass, he tells me, "We got a message from N about the rat too."

"What did he say?" N is a big deal on the West Coast, friends of ours work for him and he's someone we trust...well as much as we can trust anyone outside this house.

"It wasn't just Scarlet. There's at least one other woman but it's someone in the bureau. One of their men got wind that they picked you up today because someone told them." He pauses only a second before asking me, "Who knew?"

Adrenaline courses through my body, "Nate told the men at the bar he'd be with me." I swallow down the pissed-off feeling. "So it could be anyone." Frustration rings over me but the one thought that causes tension is that Braelynn could be lumped into that group. She could have told them and given them a heads up. I swallow the lump in my throat. "Obviously Braelynn knew but—"

"It wasn't her," Carter cuts me off with a hand on my shoulder.

"You checked her phone?" I question and shock is present in my tone but also hurt. He didn't trust her, but then again, I already knew that didn't I? Not only that, but my first thought was, when I'm back in the room, I need to check the monitoring device.

"Yeah...just to cover our bases. She didn't send a single message or make a single call. It's not her. It couldn't have been. I believe her and I trust you on this. It's not Braelynn but there is another rat."

"You believe her now?" I ask him and he only nods. Relief floods through me as Carter pours two glasses of whiskey. The crystal tumblers clink as he picks them up.

"We'll figure it out," he says and passes me mine, "we always do," he adds before clinking the glasses and downing his.

He sets his down on the counter as the amber liquid soothingly burns its way down my throat. "You tell the others?"

"Of course, they all know it wasn't her," he tells me, looking me right in the eye.

Some part of me wants to break down and stop fighting simply from knowing I've won that battle. It wasn't my naive girl. But the other part of me feels nothing but rage. "It's the same person who set her up to take the fall. I know it. I know it is."

Carter pats my shoulder again, firm and indicating agreement.

"We'll handle it tomorrow. Sleep well."

I tell him good night and stare at the whiskey bottle a little too long, realizing her name is cleared. That my brothers believe her.

I didn't realize how much I needed them to believe her until this moment. Emotions I'd rather not acknowledge swarm me as I make my way back to her, knowing all too well the war isn't over.

When I open the door, the first thing I see is her beautiful form, the second is a stack of papers.

The marriage license lays unsigned, a pen laying across it on my nightstand. As I stare at it, Braelynn turns in bed, rustling the sheets.

Pushing her hair from her face, she peers up at me through thick lashes. Her naked body is covered by only a sheet from her waist up and the comforter hugs her hips. She's tucked it between her legs and untangles herself from it.

"Declan?" she murmurs my name and I swear I'm getting used to her waking up to me hovering over her.

I close the door and tell her it's all right and to go to bed.

She groans a sweet and sexy sound as she rolls and her breasts nearly show, but the sheet still covers them. Fuck, she's so goddamn gorgeous. I'm hard instantly. I close my eyes and hold back a groan as I strip down.

"What time is it?" she asks and I let her know it's nearly 4:00 a.m.

"We should sleep in tomorrow," she says sleepily and then hugs my pillow, scooting close to my spot, as if she's waiting for me to join her. I love it. I fucking love the little things she does like that.

It doesn't change the guilt though. It only makes it grow in my chest.

I tell her, as I stand at the foot of the bed, "I'm sorry I got you into all this." My voice is low and at first, I think she hasn't heard me, but then she speaks.

"I had an idea of what I was getting into."

"If you could go back," I dare to ask her, "would you?" The bed groans as I climb in next to her.

"No. That's the part I can't get over," she murmurs, rubbing the sleep from her eyes. The raw honesty is something I didn't quite expect.

I chuckle, deep and low. "It's not funny but—"

"No it's not," she comments back although apparently my smile is contagious because she wears one too. It brightens up her face.

Smiling into the crook of her neck, I wrap my arms around her and pull her in close. "I fucking love when I make you smile," I murmur at the shell of her ear and then nip her lobe. She yelps a sweet little sound while tangling her legs with mine.

I'm naked, she's naked, and this is all I want right now.

"Spread your legs for me," I command her, kissing down her neck and she's more than eager to agree. Opening for me and wrapping her legs around my hips. Before gripping my cock, I let my thumb rub her clit and her body shivers under me.

The sight of her teeth sinking into her lip as her neck arches makes me desperate to feel her cunt wrapped around me. In one quick thrust, I'm inside of her. I don't give her time to adjust, I don't stop when she gasps or when her nails dig into my back. I fuck her like she's mine, all mine to do whatever I want with. I shove myself as far as I can inside of her, groaning into the crook of her neck as she screams out my name. Then I pound into her, over and over again, loving how she cries out each time in utter ecstasy.

She screams out my name. Mine.

"Come for me my little whore," I command her and as if my words are her undoing, she obeys. It's fucking heaven, feeling her come on my cock.

"Such a good girl," I whisper and then ravage her. Relentlessly taking her and riding through her orgasm. By the time I'm done, she's lost herself again and trembles beneath me, kissing me tenderly as I pulse inside of her.

I only get out of bed to clean up and return with a warm damp cloth to clean her up as well. She moans softly as I do and then bites down on her lip. "Settle down my little whore," I reprimand her and she smiles wider, that deep blush darkening her tanned skin.

When I get back, the license stares back at me on the nightstand. I sign it without thinking of anything other than how I feel right now.

"I need you to sign this," I tell her and put the paper on the pillow, the pen in her hand.

"Yes, husband," she says as if she's joking, but she signs it. A loopy *B* that's curved and refined, signed with a shitty ball point pen on a pillow.

She hands me the pen and paper and tells me to get into

bed. It's late and I need to sleep.

Fuck, married for not even a minute and she already has me whipped.

"Yes, wife," I respond, again somewhat comically, but my heart pounds in my chest with a feeling I've never known.

As I lay down and get comfortable, she cuddles next to me, her soft curvy body against mine, and kisses my chest. Then she tells me she loves me, and I believe her.

It occurs to me at this moment that I love her so deeply, I would light the world on fire if only she told me she wanted it to burn.

CHAPTER 17

BRAELYNN

I thought the coffee shop would be the best place to meet my mom, a dainty place on the corner of a strip that's very public, and I was right.

The sounds here are familiar and soothing. A barista steams milk for a latte, the coffee grinder whirrs, and a woman at the counter laughs.

I sit in a booth in the back corner of the café area, my hands around a mug of hot cocoa. I decide against coffee because I don't think the caffeine will do a thing to help my nervousness. My mom's mug, also filled with hot chocolate, waits across from me.

Nate glances at me from the other end of the shop and raises his eyebrows. He's not the only one guarding me today.

There are a few other men here. Declan's people. They try their best to blend in, but I know the look of them too well. They don't get lost in thought or spend too long looking at the laptops and phones they carry for cover. They're always checking to make sure I'm okay. Declan may not be here at my wishes, but with how many men he sent to stalk my every move he might as well have been.

I give Nate a thumbs-up, somewhat sarcastically, though my heart races. I don't know how this is going to go. I can already hear her telling me she's been worried sick and how disappointed she is in me for not responding to her and for making her worry.

Wait till she hears the rest.

Just as I'm swallowing down that thought, my mother sweeps in through the door of the coffee shop, pushing sunglasses onto the top of her head and patting at her hair. Her gaze runs the length of the room until she finds me, and the look of relief on her face brings me absolute shame immediately. With a loosely hanging floral sweater that nearly gets caught on a chair, she rushes through the maze of tables with her purse held tight to her side.

She barrels straight past the empty seat with the hot chocolate and leans down over me. "My baby girl," she whispers and her voice cracks. I stand up into the hug, keeping my left hand behind her back. Mom squeezes me tight, then tighter, shaking slightly.

It all adds to the guilt, but still, I hold her back just as tightly.

"Mama. Hi."

"Braelynn." Her voice is low and stressed. She pushes me back to get a good look at me, her hands gripping my shoulders, then lets out a breath. "Braelynn, where—"

"Here, sit down. I got you some cocoa."

"Cocoa? Thank you, but—" My mom lets me guide her into the seat across from me. She hooks her purse onto the chair and blinks down at the cocoa like she's never heard of it before. I take my seat and slide my hand under the table. Mom's eyes snap back to mine. "Where have you been? Ignoring all my calls and messages. Braelynn, you worried me sick, neña."

"I'm okay," I tell her simply and she leans across from me, silently looking over my expression.

She puts one hand on the table. "Where have you been? I thought I lost you. You don't have children, so you can't understand what that's like." I take a deep breath and try my best to keep my expression calm. I don't want to smile too widely and I don't want to cry just from being here with her finally, because that would worry her more. So I focus on holding myself together.

"This isn't like you. I've been up nights. I can hardly sleep. I worry about you, and I thought—"

"Mom, I have to tell you something."

Her questions stop and her eyes search mine. My mother waves me on, impatient. "Tell me, then. Explain this."

"Do you want to drink some cocoa first?"

She shakes her head, bewildered. "I can't. Tell me what you need to say."

"I've been lying to you."

Her brow furrows. She looks like she doesn't know whether to be angry or relieved or suspicious. "Lying about what?" she asks, her hands finally wrapping around that mug. Her eyes flash with worry and I wish I could skip over this part and just hug her again.

"I went away with a man." I start and my voice chokes up.

Mama startles backward, her hand going to her chest. Questions flicker through her eyes. She must be choosing between a hundred of them. Guilt weighs me down, pushing me back into the chair, when she asks, "Did he hurt you?"

"No," I whisper and the memories in my head betray the calm I wish to portray. There's a long silence. She clearly doesn't believe me so I distract her. "He made me fall in love with him, though."

My mom sags forward, looking at me with pure skepticism in her eyes. "Mi neña." A smile falters on her face. She's trying to make light of this, and I don't think she can. "So a man kept you from me?"

"Mama, I need you to listen to me."

"Neña, I'm worried for you. You lied about where you

work. Now you lied about this man. That bar isn't safe. You have to know what you're getting yourself into and now look. This man can't be—"

She keeps talking, not even pausing to take a breath. Regrets pile up on one another as tears brim in her eyes.

I regret telling her I was a waitress, but what else was I supposed to say? I had to tell her something to avoid this situation. Except I didn't avoid it in the end. I'm still sitting here in the coffee shop while my mom's cheeks redden and her voice rises a little more with every sentence.

I just need to get this out. I need her to know so we can move on from here. All the rest—the waitressing job, even being out of contact for so long that it kept her up at night—is already done. She won't ever get an explanation if she won't let me say the words. I spent hours wishing I could tell her everything.

That's what love makes people do, I think. It makes them worry and say far too much and forget that a conversation is supposed to be a two-way street.

"Mama!" I slap my hand down on the table. One of the coffee shop waiters stops mid-step on his way to us and turns around. He was probably going to ask us if we wanted to order anything to eat, but that would be a waste of time, because neither of us has taken a single sip of our cocoa and I imagine, like me, there isn't an appetite in sight.

Her eyes drop from my face to the ring on my finger. The

diamond glitters in the café light. The wedding band sits snug against the engagement ring. Both pieces in the set have been polished until they shine, and she can't miss them. I silently tell myself off for choosing my left hand to hit the table with, but...now it's done.

"Braelynn." She swallows hard. "Is that a—"

I keep my voice low and try to keep my hand from trembling. "He asked me to marry him, and I said yes." Tears come to my eyes. They're hot and stinging, and my mom hasn't had a chance to say a word, but I already know she won't approve of me being with Declan. I don't know why emotion feels thick and heavy in my chest, like it kills me that she doesn't love him already. I need her to. I need her to love him too. "I love him, Mama, and he loves me."

I swipe a napkin from the holder on the table with my right hand and dab at my eyes. *What is wrong with me?* My mom might not ever approve. That's something I thought I'd come to terms with.

It's not like I can change this. "I can't change who I love Mama," I murmur to her, attempting to hold myself together but her wide eyes only stare back with uncertainty before landing on the ring again. My mind whirls with all the things I wish I could tell her and I find myself breathing heavier and heavier.

My mom stares at the ring, a frown marring her face. It's only then that I notice the dark circles under her eyes and the way her grays show more than ever. I can't tell what she's thinking at all.

"That..." Her hand inches toward mine, but she doesn't actually touch me. "That ring is expensive, neña."

I can see the puzzle pieces slipping into place in her mind as the seconds tick by. I dare to whisper, "He could afford it just fine."

Her eyes come back to mine, and now I see her hope and her fear. That's a tough combination. "Who is this man?"

I steel myself. This is the part that worried me more than anything. Getting married without her knowing about it was one thing. Marrying the man I chose... "Declan Cross."

"No," she whispers, and her hand flutters at her throat. My mom glances around the coffee shop as if she's hoping no one else heard. Like it doesn't have to be true if no one else knows.

"Yes," I tell her and my heart breaks into a million pieces. "I love him and he loves me."

Her eyes finally land on mine, and now we're both teary-eyed. "Not my baby girl." Her voice wavers and it utterly destroys me.

"I knew you wouldn't approve," I swallow thickly, barely able to keep it together. I glance past my mother and see the men watching. They all know. I hate this. I hate all of this.

"Tell me it isn't true, Braelynn," my mother says, her accent slightly thicker with her growing emotions.

I sit up straight and wipe at my eyes again. The tears just keep coming no matter what I do, so I don't have a choice but to wipe them away. At least my voice is steady when I speak. "He loves me."

"He's dangerous." My mother whispers *dangerous* like she's worried she might be overheard by Declan himself. She doesn't realize that his people are all around us in this café. Even if they weren't, I sleep in his bed every night. I know how dangerous he and his brothers are. I've known for a long time.

"They're all dangerous, Mama. Every man I've ever loved." My blood runs cold knowing this is exactly what I expected. Knowing I couldn't change this with all the money and power in the world. Some men are always feared, and who would want their daughter to be with a man like him? If she knew our entire story, she'd take me away from him in a heartbeat. That's what hurts the most. I know she has good reason to want to keep me from him. I know how bad it can get. And yet, I still love him.

My mom shakes her head, her lips quivering. I don't want her to sob at the table. I don't want her fears to be so overwhelming that she won't see me. She can't think so little of me, can she? She can't think I'd throw my life away on someone I didn't love.

"I love him. Please. Please, Mama." I reach out and take her hand, clasping it tight on top of the table. "Please just give him a chance."

"You have no idea what you're getting into with those men, mi neña."

"Unfortunately, I do." I lift another napkin to wipe at my eyes. I've gone through three of them already, and the tears are starting to slow, thank God. Because there's more to tell her. I have to be honest with my mother if I'm going to have her in my life. "It wasn't just a proposal. We're married already because of..." Now I'm the one glancing around the coffee shop to be sure we're not overheard. Of course, there's always a chance. "Because of some of those things."

My heart races as she holds my hand tighter and her face crumples with worry.

"I'm okay, and I love him, but this"—I lift my hand so the ring shines in the light— "this couldn't wait."

With my limited confession, she's beside herself, really. As if she's blaming herself for missing all the signs with me. As if there's some solution to the fact that I'm married to Declan, and she's just not seeing it. She looks like she's running out of time, and that makes my heart clench, because I know that feeling very well.

"He cares for me."

Her hand wraps around mine and I can see her will cave slightly, although I'm not sure to what extent.

"You're married?" she says as if it's a question but it's not.

"Yes," I answer quietly, feeling the tension shift slightly.

My mother blinks away the tears and noticeably calms herself.

"I'm married and I'm happy that I am."

My words bring her gaze to me and she stares me down like she's done before. As if she's testing to see if I'm telling her the truth. "I mean it," I reaffirm, "I love him, Mama."

Mama watches me very carefully when I say these words. I look back at her, my gaze unwavering. I'm telling her the truth, and she needs to know that. "I want you to meet him."

"Well." A nervous laugh. I'm not sure if there's relief now, or if she's simply going along so she doesn't lose me entirely. "Do I have a choice?"

It's another half-joke that breaks my heart.

"Mama, please. When I tell you I love him, I mean it."

For a few seconds, she looks exactly the same. Afraid. Haunted. Guilty. But gradually, her expression softens. When she looks into my eyes, I can tell she's really seeing me.

"You really love him?"

"Yes." I nod, then dab at the corners of my eyes again.

"Then I will meet him."

"You will?" I ask her again to make sure. I'm quick to grab her hand and squeeze, and she squeezes mine back. I know she's still worried. I know, honestly, that she has a right to be worried. But if she's willing to meet Declan, then there's hope.

"I'm so happy," I tell her even though I know I must look like I'm on the verge of tears again.

"I will meet your husband," she says, more firmly. Then she pats my hand. "Has this cocoa been sitting here long?"

I shrug. "Fifteen minutes, maybe?"

"It's a little cold." She waves at the waiter, who makes his way over with a relieved smile. "We'll get something stiffer. And then you'll tell me everything, won't you?" she asks me, staring me down once again.

I look my mother dead in the eyes, a small smile on my face while I lie to her, "I'll tell you everything."

CHAPTER 18

DECLAN

There's something we're missing and it's driving me mad. I toss the fucking book on Carter's desk. My older brother eyes me warily. It's fucking late and I should be in bed with Braelynn, but I can't fucking sleep.

I've flipped through every page of the notebook and there was someone else working with Scarlet. Someone who knew a female cop and reported to her. I've watched every security video with Scarlet on repeat until my eyes feel as if they're bleeding. Every video with my Braelynn.

It doesn't fucking make sense. None of it. It's as if I must be staring at the fucking rat and yet he's hidden.

It would be so easy to simply get rid of the detective. And everyone he's worked with. I have a list...but I'm all too aware at least one name is missing.

"Who the fuck do we have to torture to figure it out?"

"The female cop is gone. N got a hold of her with the issue he's going through," Carter murmurs. He has his intel and I have mine. She would have been the only lead to the name. Even this detective doesn't know how she got her information. Which is partly a blessing. Hearsay isn't enough to grant an arrest warrant.

"The only info he gave me is what I told you last night."

I clear my throat, breathing in deeply. "And I'm guessing he didn't get a name."

"If he did, he didn't tell me."

The domino pieces slip into place in my mind. The judge, the detective who works with the feds, the cops beneath him, and then the rats. There is Scarlet, but then there's someone else. I find myself questioning if it was Scarlet who set Braelynn up or one of my men.

"You're overthinking this," Carter murmurs. "We get rid of the cops and the rat is left with no one to squeal to," he tells me, his dark eyes piercing into mine. "We'll find out who it is eventually. They always tell on themselves."

He doesn't get it. I don't have the patience for this. I don't have the mercy or grace. I can barely focus on anything else.

"There's got to be something we're missing," I tell him. "Someone framed Braelynn."

"Well if it wasn't Scarlet...then...then someone else told

the cops the export numbers. The, what was it, 886 thousand, which is damn well high enough for federal prosecution of embezzlement."

Jase corrects him, "It was under 850...like 849 k. That's how much was on her sheet."

A chill goes down my spine. "That's not right. Hold on, that's not right."

Jase's brow furrows, "What's not right? Those are the numbers reported."

"It shouldn't be, it's not what was on her sheet."

"Jase, where did you get those figures from?" I question him although I can barely hear my own voice, the ringing in my head is so loud.

"It doesn't matter, does it? It was made up."

"No, it does. On the video."

"Go back. Go back to when we first met about Braelynn. About her sneaking around in the office."

"What date was it?" he questions and I rattle it off. I know all these details by fucking heart now.

"You said those numbers. Those figures. They're not what I put down though." Every piece of footage, every person, every possibility races through my mind.

My brothers and I are the ones who discussed what I would put on those sheets for her. But the figures said out loud weren't exactly the figures I put in the sheet. It was random. It wasn't supposed to be a real test. I trusted her, and it was only to ease their concerns.

My entire body turns to ice. "No one but us," I start and then realize someone could have been in the security room. Carter doesn't object as I click through files upon files of security footage, until I find the folder with the date we met.

"It was Nate who said 886 thousand was reported," Jase says and my head whirls as I swallow thickly. Hitting play on the hall video just outside the security room in the bar. My brothers and I would be in the back room of the bar. Discussing my new obsession with Braelynn and my plan to ensure she wasn't a rat. And there he is...in front of all of our eyes.

"So, you said Nate told you?" Carter questions Jase.

Nate unlocks the security room and I speed up the tape. He doesn't leave for two hours.

"Why the fuck would Nate tell you any other figure than what was reported? And how the hell would he get the same number we discussed?"

Nate would have heard our conversation. He would have heard my plans. He would have known what was going to happen and that she could so very easily be set up.

My vision turns red as my brothers discuss the reality. And all I can envision is wrapping my hands around that rat bastard's neck.

He listened to the conversation. He set her up. But the figures he remembered weren't the ones that were reported. He could have seen the spreadsheet before it was given to her, he could have watched me set it up from that office, and he could have written them down.

What he remembered was what we said though...he really did fucking tell on himself.

I stare at the computer as he exits the security room, a goddamn notepad in his hand. My blood races through my veins and adrenaline screams through me. Fucking Nate?

How could he do this? It makes no fucking sense at all.

Carter interrupts my thoughts as rage builds upon rage as the betrayal sets in. Nate? My right-hand man? Why? He fucking drove her home the other day. He was alone with her. My vision turns red.

"Nate was working with the female cop. Was he working with anyone else? If he wasn't, there's a good chance he will be shortly now that she's gone."

CHAPTER 19

BRAELYNN

I've never done this before and I'm nervous as hell because it feels like a different kind of test entirely. I keep turning the ring around my finger and I wish I wouldn't. It's an obvious sign of my nerves. So instead, I tuck my hands inside of the long sleeves of my blue knit sweater so only the tips of my fingers show.

I've never been here either and it occurs to me that the room was designed for just this. The office is small and cozy and just off the kitchen, with a couch, a chair, and a desk. Aria's art hangs on walls painted a warm eggshell color. I think this room would feel warm even on the coldest day of the year. Built-in shelves on one side hold smaller pieces by Aria and photographs. She and Carter smile out from one.

The two of them plus the kids.

It's a heartbreakingly normal home office. A stranger sitting in here would know that somebody liked art, and that Aria and Carter are happy together. They'd never know what it takes to win happiness for people like Carter and his brothers. All that darkness would be hidden from them.

Or, if not hidden, just...out of sight. It's not on display here, the way it might be if Aria put it into one of her pieces. Well except for the fact that the person staring back at me is supposed to hear all of that...since she's a therapist.

I settle back into the couch, unsure of what, exactly, to do with my body. This room is neutral in a way that says it's trying to be neutral, which is very different from the rest of the house. I know there are cameras here. I know I'm being watched.

Which isn't what I'd expect from a therapy session, I guess, but it is what I'd expect in the world of the Cross brothers.

"This isn't a test, right?" My soft question moves across the room, no doubt being picked up by microphones from those cameras. How many people are tracking the words that come out of my mouth? Just Declan, or one of his men, or one of his brothers? Is there a room somewhere in the house where they can sit and watch? Anxiousness creeps up my arms and I find myself crossing them as I breathe out a slow steady breath.

I don't like the thought of a dark room and computer

screens displaying my therapy session, but I bet there's an explanation for that, too. There's a reason it has to happen.

The therapist smiles at me from her seat near the desk. She's an older woman, and she looks at home in this office. An elegant top is paired with slacks that look both comfortable and expensive at the same time. Dark hair is pulled back in a twist. If the cameras make her feel anything, I can't tell. She meets my eyes with a warm, considering expression. "Are you used to being tested?"

I glance around the room one more time, still unsure of all of this as I readjust. I didn't expect for the session to be totally private, obviously, but it would be easier if I knew where the cameras were. If this kind of thing is going to be a regular part of my life, then there's no need to hide it so much. He can be up-front about it.

"Braelynn?" Her question directs my attention back to her, and I remember that she asked me a question in return for mine.

"I can tell you anything? Declan said I could, and can I trust him with that?" I ask her. He can watch all he wants while I spill out everything that comes to mind.

Afterall, he told me to say whatever I wanted. I'm tempted to do just that, but...I want her confirmation first. I know that's not enough to truly judge a person on, but I have Aria's word that she's good, too.

"Of course you can. I mean that. Anything." She leans

forward a little, folding her hands over a notepad in her lap. "I grew up in this life, Braelynn. You can tell me you murdered your first lover and I wouldn't say a word to anyone."

Declan told me that, too. This woman has been around for years. I let myself relax a little and remember her first question.

"Yes. I'm used to being tested."

She sits up, taking a pen in hand. "It sounds like you don't like that."

"I hated it. I was furious about it."

"In the past, or do you still feel that way?"

"I feel like—" I give it a few moments. There's no need to rush my answers. "It was upsetting, and it made me angry. I didn't understand it, and that just made me feel...out of control."

"What changed?"

I shrug, a bit helpless at how to answer. "It was gradual. I had to take the time to figure things out. The hardest thing to get past was the distrust."

"Have you communicated this with Declan?"

"Yes."

"What was his response?"

"He was remorseful. He felt awful about it." An ache in my chest reminds me of how much I love him. Of how it hurts to think of him terrified for me, and worried, and how that must still follow him around to this day. "He does his best to reassure me. Every chance he gets now."

She absorbs this for a few minutes. It's clear that she's had lots of experience as a therapist because there's no impatience in the quiet. There really is space for me to say anything I need to say.

When I don't continue, she gives a small nod. "Do you forgive him?"

I do. I could tell her right away, but I force myself to slow down and think through the question from beginning to the end. Sometimes, I don't want to feel my feelings. I want to push them away and get on with my life. That's not why I'm here today.

But, when I've thought about it again, I come to the same conclusion as before.

"Yes. I do." Emotion makes my chest feel tight all over again. Normally I'd cry, then pull myself together. Or I'd push it away and ignore it. I let myself feel it. "I forgive him. I love him, and I understand why it happened. But it still scares me."

"Still scares you? Worse than before, or—"

"Not as much."

"Because?"

"Because they believe me." Isn't it crazy how much we rely on others to not feel crazy?

The therapist nods. I didn't need her to back me up—I'm confident that Declan and his brothers believe me.

"What do they believe you about?"

"I don't want to talk about it." The defensive feeling takes me by surprise. So does my tone, which is way more forceful than I mean. So much for taking my time with my answers.

The therapist raises her hands, still calm. "That's fine. Is that a trigger for you?"

"A trigger?"

"Bringing up whatever it was that happened." She lowers her hands slowly, like she doesn't want to startle me.

"Yes." My face is hot, and emotions bubble under the surface. I want to brush it off so badly, but then...this is why I'm talking to a therapist in the first place. I tried to sweep all of this under the rug, and it's just not happening. "Kind of."

"Does Declan know that?" This question is calm and gentle, just like the therapist, and it makes me feel better that we're not talking about what happened, exactly, but the way I've handled it. That's...safer ground, but it does make me think I should eventually talk through all of it, even if I don't want to.

And I don't want to.

"I feel like he does," I offer because I'm not sure what he knows. I don't live in his mind. If I did, we probably wouldn't have had so much trouble with the testing.

"Maybe it's something you can express to him," the therapist suggests. "I find creating a strong boundary around what is acceptable to be exposed to and discussed and what isn't is very helpful in this life."

The conversation continues easily for another forty minutes. But I keep going back to the boundaries and how it's so very obvious now that I think about it. Declan is searching for mine so he doesn't cross them.

A soft knock at the door interrupts my thoughts.

"Yes?" the therapist calls out.

The door opens, and Declan pokes his head in. "Should I join, or no?" He runs a hand over the back of his neck, glancing at me. "Just offering, if you want." His stubbled jaw is still the same sharpness it's always been, yet there's nothing about him that intimidates me anymore. Seeing him, those piercing eyes searching mine, there's nothing I want more than to be in his arms. I shake my head. "It's okay. I think we're done for now."

I stand, content on ending the session and the therapist follows my lead. She faces me with a smile. "Let me know if you want to talk again, Braelynn. I'm available. All it takes is a phone call."

She steps past me, and Declan moves out of her way. He doesn't follow her, though. He stands in the doorway, stopping me from leaving. My stomach drops at the expression on his face. Something's wrong. It's only then that I remember the fucking cameras and that all of this was probably nothing more than a test. It's a crippling realization.

"I have some things to tell you, my sweet girl." That same remorseful look fills his eyes, and a chill runs down my spine.

I swallow thickly, wanting to get it over with. "Did I say something I shouldn't have?"

He blinks, his brow furrowing. "What?"

"I assumed you were watching. Cameras, or—I assumed someone was watching, anyway."

"No, Brae." He takes a step toward me. "I didn't watch, and no one will. These sessions are for you. There aren't any cameras in here."

"Oh." My laugh sounds nervous. It sounds exactly how I feel. "It's...something else, then."

"Something else," he agrees. "It's something I think you're going to want to know, and it might help you get a little closure."

His eyes darken as he speaks, and his skin flushes. He was remorseful before, but now he's angry. He might've been relaxed and curious when he first knocked on the door. Now he's definitely not. His shoulders are tense. He's on edge.

My heart beats faster. "I get scared when you're like this."

I'm met with another confused look. "Like what?"

"You're on edge. Your mind is elsewhere. You're angry and a minute ago you were...well, you were calm a minute ago, and now...are you angry?"

A sad yet handsome smirk lifts his lips up. "My naive girl," he says in that tone that melts every worry. He moves in closer and strokes a hand over my hair. I'm comforted by the gesture in spite of myself. Declan, when he's like this, is actually a dangerous man. I'm not wrong to be wary. "You have no idea the fucked-up shit I'm thinking right now."

"Should I be worried?"

His hand settles on the side of my neck, and Declan bends to whisper into my ear. The warm caress of his breath makes me shiver. I wouldn't mind if he took me to bed for this conversation, whatever it's going to be. I wouldn't mind hiding in the blankets with him.

"I found out who set you up," he whispers.

It takes a moment for me to realize exactly what he said. Cold sweeps over every inch of my body.

I gasp, my trembling hands coming up to touch his shirt. I don't need him to stand on my own two feet. I just want to be touching him. My body steadies the second my palms are over his heartbeat. I dare to ask him, "What are you going to do?"

He chuckles, and the sound is low and hot. It's dangerous, just like he is. Sometimes, when we're in bed together, I can forget about the dark parts of Declan. I can ignore the dark parts of both our lives. But they're always with him.

My heart pounds. Whatever Declan's about to say, he's already decided. He knew before he came into this room. He has a plan for what happens next, and knowing Declan, it's not going to be a lawsuit or a cease-fire.

"I'm going to make him pay," he says, his voice just above a whisper. Shivers explode down my spine, all the way down the backs of my legs and down to my toes. This isn't just Declan speaking to me now. This is Declan Cross. "I'm going to set an example. No one will ever touch you or speak ill of you ever again. And I want you to come with me."

CHAPTER 20

DECLAN

My sweet naive girl doesn't belong in Carter's office.

With a pretty blue knit sweater that makes her appear even smaller, she's out of place in the harsh and dark atmosphere.

I thread my fingers between hers and squeeze. Our clasped hands hang between the two chairs. She sits on the left and I sit on the right. Both of us are across from Carter, who's barely looked at me while he apologizes to Braelynn.

"There's nothing we can do to make it right," Carter says as his thumb taps against the desk.

"It's okay," Braelynn is quick to say, and I swear I can hear her heart pounding.

"It's not okay," Carter corrects her but in a gentler tone I appreciate. "He's going to pay Braelynn, and we have a plan."

I bring her knuckles to my lips and kiss them one by one. "Don't be scared."

"I do have some questions," Carter states, and I breathe in deeply.

"Like a test?" she asks and the hesitancy and fear are still there. Disappointment flows through me. Not toward her but toward myself.

"No more tests; I really did a number on you," I tell her, my thumb running soothing circles over her knuckles.

"I read the note that you left here...when," Carter attempts to be careful with his words. I've only seen him like this a few times and it's only ever been toward my sisters-in-law. It's an odd feeling to realize he sees her as she truly is. Family. To care for and to protect, even from us.

"When I ran away," Braelynn completes his thought in a whisper.

"You were scared when you ran?" he asks and my shoulders stiffen.

"She was terrified." Adrenaline pumps harder as I think about what comes next. "For

good reason." Carter only stares at me for a moment, he doesn't respond.

"Did something specific happen that made you that afraid? Or was it a thought or something you remembered, maybe?"

"Can I ask why?" Her chest rises and falls.

"Of course you can," I answer for him. "You can ask whatever you need."

"Because you accepted blame for something I don't think you did."

"At that point," she answers with her eyes glassy, "I thought I must have...I overheard something and it—"

"What did you overhear?" Carter asks before I can get the question out.

"I overheard something—" Her gaze drops and I tell her it's all right.

"Hey, hey," I murmur and reach over, cupping her jaw in my hand. "It's okay," I console her. Her hands reach up to grab my wrists.

"It doesn't feel okay."

"It's better than okay, my sweet girl. We're ending this and every piece of this today."

"You promise?" she questions, hope in her eyes that reminds me of all the times she looked up at me, wanting me to be her hero when I'm nothing more than a villain.

"I promise," I tell her and I lean forward, planting a gentle kiss on her lips. She molds her lips to mine and clings to me. I don't want to break the bond but I must.

As my heart pounds in my chest and I pull away, her eyes stay closed longer, as if she doesn't want that moment to end.

"You overheard what? From who?" Carter asks as I sit back in my seat.

Braelynn breathes out slowly, not looking at Carter but staring at the desk as if it's replaying a memory. "Nate was on the front porch and he said...he said something like 'You're sure it is Braelynn? I don't want to be the one to do it this time.'"

"Sure what was you?" Carter asks and confusion deepens the crease in his forehead.

Braelynn shakes her head. "I don't know. It sounded like he was saying I sent something. That someone was sure I sent something. I didn't send anything to anyone," she blurts out the words, her voice raising higher and higher. "He said the bitch sent it."

"The bitch he referred to might have been the cop?" I question, looking at Carter who nods along with me. "The cop sent him something about Braelynn?"

"Probably the warrant for her arrest," Carter comes to the conclusion.

"What?" Braelynn questions.

She glances between the two of us and her grip on my hand gets tighter. "I assumed I was the woman he was talking about. He did say my name."

"Is it possible the conversation was about someone else who mentioned you?" Carter asks, and Braelynn's expression makes it obvious she's thinking back on it all.

"Nate's been working with the cops."

"Oh my God," she breathes, her eyes widening.

"He's the one who set you up. He could have been talking

about the cop he was working with."

"Can you remember exactly what he said?"

She shakes her head, her breathing intensifying. "I don't think I want to think about it." My poor girl is spiraling and I can't watch it happen. Nate's hurt her enough for this life. No more. He doesn't get to keep hurting her like this. That's the thing about abuse. Even when the abuser's gone, the pain stays in the memories.

"Okay then. It's done. Braelynn it's done," Carter says at the same time that I tell her, "You don't need to answer anything else. It's over Braelynn."

"It doesn't matter what exactly he said. We know enough of the pieces," Carter says with finality.

Her hands tremble in mine and I hold her while Carter gets her a drink. The glass clinks in the background while I tell her repeatedly that it's all right. Whiskey, of course, which she only stares at a second before she gulps it down.

"I think I can offer you something that will end it all for you," I add as I stare deep into her eyes, knowing this is something I would want but also knowing I'm fucked in the head and she isn't me. She isn't damaged and brutal like I am. "Real closure and justice."

"I want that," she answers desperately. "I want it to be done with forever."

"Come with us," Carter says, already making his way to the door.

CHAPTER 21

BRAELYNN

I'm as nervous as I've ever been in my life as we walk through the house toward a certain wing that I'd rather avoid forever. My heart beats rapidly in my chest. My palms sweat. My legs feel heavy, like they might take over and run me right back to Declan's bedroom without my permission. Declan is steady at my side, his expression determined.

"Declan," I say, my voice shaking. "I don't know if I can—"

He puts a hand on my lower back and adds the slightest pressure to tell me to keep walking. "You're with me, and I love you. Nothing is going to happen to you. I'm sorry anyone ever hurt you, Braelynn. That ends for good today."

From behind me, Carter cuts in. "This is a gift to you."

"I—" I shake my head.

"If you don't want to do this," Carter continues. "You don't have to. It's—"

"She's going to want this," Declan says, cutting his brother off. "I don't want her to live with regret or ever wonder where we stand."

"Why would I want this?" I ask Declan, my pulse racing even faster as we pass one door and then another, both of which are metal.

He glances down at me and a muscle in the side of his jaw tics. "He hurt you. This all happened because of him."

I dare to ask the question, half expecting to see a dead body behind whatever door is opened. "Is he still alive?"

Dark anger flashes through his eyes. "Not for long."

It hits me then that I'm going to witness a murder. That I'll see this man die in just a moment. And I'm so torn on how to feel. So conflicted by right and wrong. Memories fly through my mind and with Nate, come memories of Scarlet. I nearly trip over my own feet as I'm led to a closed door ahead.

"Come on, Brae. I want you to see what happens to anyone who ever hurts you."

The heavy metal door opens and just inside the door, Nate's tied to a chair with thick ropes and has a black bag over his head. Jase stands at his side, his arms crossed over his chest, a scowl on his face.

Shock and fear both race through me.

When we're all inside the room, Jase pulls the bag off.

Nate's gagged, his face red, and his eyes wide with fear. His lip is cut and his cheek bruised. My breath catches and I can barely stand up straight.

Jase removes the gag and Nate's head lulls. He's barely holding on to consciousness.

"Get anything from him?"

"He admitted he was working with a cop. He made a deal."

"I was," Nate exhales breathlessly.

"He was covering his ass."

"According to his bank account he was covering more than just his ass," Daniel speaks up from the corner of the room. I didn't even see him there. He stalks forward, wearing all black, just like Jase.

My stomach turns. Cold races up and down my arms. The memory of what he did is as clear and vivid as if it had happened five minutes ago. The way he killed...

"Scarlet," I whisper.

"Scarlet was working for the other side, Braelynn," Carter says. "But she was also working with Nate, wasn't she?"

"Wasn't she?" he repeats.

Nate's breathing is hard and fast, and he works his jaw like it's painful from the way they gagged him. "She's a liar," he says, his tone urgent. "Whatever she told you isn't true."

My heart races as his bloodshot eyes meet mine.

Is he calling me a liar? Betrayal and fear creep into my mind with racing questions. I didn't lie about anything. I don't know anything about any of this. My throat tightens and I can't speak.

Carter brushes by my side and goes to pace around Nate. There's so much raw fear in the room that I can taste it in the air. Anger, too. The brothers are furious, and they're scary when they're furious.

"It didn't come from Braelynn," Carter tells Nate. He and Jase are both circling Nate now, and Nate's eyes follow them with wide-eyed terror. "She had no idea until just a moment ago."

Jase pulls out a leather sleeve. I can see the handles of three different knives poking out from the top. My mouth goes dry, and my heartbeat is painful now. I don't think it's supposed to beat this fast under any circumstance.

"Don't," says Nate. "Don't do this to me."

Jase stares at him, cold and blank, then comes over to me. "You have choices."

"No." I shake my head, maybe a little harder than I needed to. "I don't...I don't want to do that." I involuntarily take a step back.

I don't want to torture a person. I know that Nate's not good. I know he did this to us. But I don't want that memory in Declan's mind, and I don't want it in mine, either.

Declan takes my hand in his. In his other, he offers me a gun. The metal is cold and heavy in my palm. "Take this my sweet girl," he whispers at my neck.

My heart races and I'm all too aware that they're all watching me, even though I can't move my gaze from the death stare Nate has locked onto me.

I want to shake my head and deny that, too, but instead, I take it.

My body is heavy as he raises my arm for me, helping me to hold the weapon.

"You can make the decision," Declan says, softly. This is the same way he tells me that he loves me. He reassures me all the while Nate shakes his head, cursing, and telling them they're making a mistake.

"It wasn't me," Nate insists. He wriggles in the ropes like there's any hope of getting free. There's not. They tied him too tight. "You've got the wrong guy."

"We don't," Jase says, his tone flat.

"No, we fucking don't," Carter agrees. "We know it was you. We have plenty of proof. You knew there would be consequences if we found out."

"You can end this," Declan tells me, his front to my back. His heart beats steadily and his voice is so calm. "This is the man who set you up," he tells me as I stare at Nate, remembering how he stood there when they lowered me into the tub.

"He knew you had nothing to do with it. He fucking knew," Declan tells me and the anger in his words tightens his tone. My eyes prick with tears as the memories come back to me, one at a time, each of them playing out.

It's wrong to kill, but it's not so black and white, is it? Not in this world, not with what's happened.

There are shades of gray in everything.

"It wasn't me," Nate says, a little louder.

Jase moves around him again and holds up the case full of knives. "You sure you don't want to get his confession?"

"No," Declan says behind me and I feel like I'm hovering outside my body. "He'll lie his way into hell. There's no point."

Declan moves around behind me, his strong hands sliding over my arms until his hands cover mine. Both of us raise the gun together, but it's mostly me. He lets me be the one to carry more of the weight. He's just supporting me.

I don't pull the trigger though. My heart thumps, and I know I should. I know deep inside a part of me will always be terrified until this man is dead and gone. My finger doesn't move though.

"Okay," Declan murmurs into my ear as tears slip down my heated cheeks. "You can put it down if you want. I mean that, Brae. We'll shoot him for you. We'll end him for you."

"No," Nate yells, his voice sharpening. "You got the wrong guy. It wasn't me. Why can't you see that? It's not me! I'm not the one who fucked you over!"

Declan moves his finger up to hover over mine. Our fingers are arranged above the trigger, neither of us touching it yet. "Whenever you're ready," he tells me and I can barely hear him over the rushing of the blood in my ears.

"What the fuck." Nate laughs, and it's a wild, terrified sound. "I can't fucking believe you, Braelynn. You're a fucking liar. You just wanted to take a shot at me, and this is how you're going to do it. You're a goddamn—"

Rage flashes through me, hot as anything I've ever felt. "I never lied," I tell him, my voice rising above his bullshit, and then I pull the trigger. *Bang!*

Once and then twice. "I'm not a liar!" It doesn't take much pressure at all. So little pressure, actually, that I keep firing. Nate slumps in the chair, but I don't stop shooting. Blood seeps out of each hole so slowly. My hands shake as I fire again.

Declan stands at my back, his arms strong and steady on mine. If I faltered, he'd catch me. I don't, though. I'm breathing hard, the rush of air painful, but I'm not falling.

I keep firing until the gun clicks in my hand. All the bullets are gone.

I lower the gun, pointing it to the ground, as my ragged breathing slowly calms.

Nate doesn't move. He's still. Dead. He'll never do anything to any of us again. "It's over," Declan says, reaching for the gun.

Numbly, I hand the gun off to Declan.

It takes me a moment of standing there, realizing what happened before I can straighten my back and know that it's over.

"You okay?" Declan asks, tipping my chin up.

I look him in the eye and tell him, "I don't want to be involved." My voice is loud enough that his brothers can hear, and I want them to. I don't want anyone to be confused about how my life is going to be going forward. "In any of this. Ever again."

"Okay," Declan says with a half smirk. "Do you feel...does it feel like—"

"I'm happy he's dead," I rush the words out, not recognizing the person I am as I look over to Nate's blood-soaked chest. I swallow thickly. "It feels like it's over," I tell Declan and then I turn and walk out of the room without another glance in Nate's direction.

I feel Jase and Carter's eyes on me. There's a moment of dead silence as I leave the room.

Footsteps follow me into the hall, and then Declan's hands are on me. He shoves me into the wall and kisses me, his lips hot on mine. His tongue is possessive in my mouth. He nips at my lip and kisses me deeper, his whole body leaning toward mine.

The heat is all consuming. The need for him to take all of this away by putting his body on mine.

The tension from before is gone. I kiss him back with everything I have. It's a strange lightness that takes over. I never wanted to have to kill anyone, but in a way, it's like taking my own life back. Nobody else can have it. All that matters now is Declan.

He pulls back, and pride shines in his eyes. He looks over my face and comes in for another deep kiss before he can speak. "I fucking love you."

I slide my hands around his neck, feeling his pulse along the way. Declan's warm and soft and alive, and mine. No one can ever tell me differently.

"Is it…" I'm emotional. Choked up over the way he looks right now. Over the relief I feel, and that he must feel, too. "Is it over now?"

He huffs out a laugh. "There are things I need to take care of. But for you? All of this is done. It's over, Brae. You never want to deal with any of this again, you don't have to."

"I don't."

"I love you so fucking much." Declan bends down and kisses me and I don't know if it's the adrenaline or the relief or just his hands on mine telling me everything I've wanted to hear since it all started.

"I just want you to love me," I murmur and press myself into him.

He cracks a devilishly charming smile that makes my heart skip a beat. Declan has always been hot, breathtakingly handsome, but there's something about the way he smiles that makes me fall even harder for him. He presses a gentle kiss to my forehead as his hands tighten around my waist.

He's still very, very close, like he can't pull himself away.

"Then," he says, "all you have to do now is love me back."

I rise up on tiptoes and kiss him again. This is the taste of the man I love. The man I'm going to love for the rest of my life. He makes everything worth it. "I can do that."

His hands roam my body and before I can stop myself, I'm pressing my lips to his with a greater need than I've felt before.

He groans deep in his throat as his thumbs hook the waistline of my pants, tugging ever so slightly. As my body heats and my heart races for more, he pulls back, but only to look over his shoulder.

Just as I think he'll deny me, that it's utterly insane to want him after what just happened, he tugs my hand, says "Come here," and leads me to a short hallway.

Before I can look around or question anything, his lips are on mine.

He presses my back against the wall and his fingers drift up my shirt. His touch is both demanding and gentle, both sides of this man I love. He takes from me in a way that fills me with a deep need for more. I could never have enough of this man.

Hips press against mine and his tongue sweeps against mine before he nips my bottom lip and then murmurs for me to turn around. It's a heady feeling, when desire takes over and I give in to it, doing everything he tells me.

"You'll be quiet, my naïve girl," he tells me as he unbuckles his pants and then pulls mine down. "Won't you?" he questions at the shell of my ear, sending delicate shivers down my spine and pebbling my nipples. The head of his cock plays at my entrance and I would agree to whatever he demanded.

I curve my back for him as I nod my head and answer, "Yes, Declan."

In a single thrust, he's inside of me. The quick sting of sweet pain and impending pleasure force a gasp from me. As I brace myself against the wall, he fucks me relentlessly. It's all too much too fast and yet at the same time, I need more.

I need all of him. As if answering my unspoken desire, his left hand sweeps under my shirt and bra, cupping and kneading my breast. He pinches my nipple at the same time that he nips the curve of my neck. The pleasure rises and it takes everything in me to be as quiet as I can be as he fucks me with a hunger I've never felt before. Murmuring how I'm his good girl and that he loves me.

Chapter 22

Declan

"One rat down...the rest of them need to go too," I mutter to my brother as we drive along the gravel road to an old house by the river. This place used to be an escape, a rundown shack in the middle of nowhere. No one would find us here when we were kids. We were trying to figure shit out without going back home where our father was waiting and slowly killing himself with alcohol.

Until we did get found. A cocky smirk lifts my lips as I take in the dilapidated place. "My first arrest happened right there." I point to the cracked concrete front steps, remembering how scared I was and knowing that the cop only lived another month after those cuffs were locked around my wrist.

Carter puts the car in park and Jase pipes up from the

back seat, "Good times."

Rough chuckles from the four of us fill the cab of the car.

They're quickly silenced as my phone pings. "They're almost here," I tell my brothers, reading the message from the tracker on the back of the detective's car.

I knew he wouldn't be able to resist. So we used Nate's phone to respond to the waiting messages. Detective Mauer is expecting an exchange tonight. He's planning on arresting Nate and me and helping Nate get out of the mess he got into. He said he'd give him a deal. This isn't a plan to take us down, it's a plan to get Nate out. Too bad for the good detective, Nate is already dead and Mauer's about to join him.

"How many are with him?" Carter asks.

"He'd be stupid to come without back up, even if he thinks it's just Declan and Nate." Daniel answers.

It's not enough to get rid of one bad apple, so to speak. That cop who arrested me years ago came down for a drug bust and stumbled on something bigger. He had to go, but no one else was involved. Over time, that changed. Like the shit we're dealing with now. There were six total. The first two were Scarlet and Nate. Next the female cop N took care of who was working with Nate.

That leaves the detective and two cops that were working with Scarlet.

"I hope both," I comment to Carter. They know damn well they shouldn't, we have orders against them, but he's hungry and pissed off and that detective doesn't mind breaking rules.

If they come with him, they won't report it. Which only makes it easier for us to get rid of the bodies without worry.

I roll the window down as we sit in the car, counting down the minutes while Jase and Daniel load up their guns before heading out. It's dark and there's plenty of brush for them to hide behind. Two of us will be seated in the car. Carter, with his hood up, could be anyone, certainly could look like Nate driving me to a meet that doesn't exist, setting me up for an arrest.

The back car doors shut and I'm left alone with a cold breeze, the taste for vengeance. My brother is to my left, holding his Glock in his hand and allowing the sounds of the night to drift in.

"We might get all three in one go," Carter murmurs.

I hum an affirmative response. "It'd be too fucking easy. Be done with it and get back home before Brae gets into bed." The idea quirks my lips up even though my heart pounds and every muscle in me coils with the adrenaline that hasn't quit all day.

"We trashing the cars?" I ask Carter, already thinking about what's next. The tracker goes off on my phone.

"Wipe it and dump it into the river," Carter answers as he pulls his hood up and then reaches into the glove compartment for another gun.

I smirk at him. "One for each hand?"

He lets out a laugh as the cars pull up behind us. One's the detective. The other is a cop car. Both of us stay still as can be. "Never can be too careful," he says ever so eerily as red, white, and blue flash.

"Come out with your hands up," the voice over the speaker is heard clear enough. The two cops stay back, I watch in the side mirror as our detective gets out of his car but stays behind the door. The voice comes back, one of the other cops, those poor fuckers, "I repeat, step out of your vehicle and come out with your hands up."

Neither Carter nor I move. My heart thumps loud and heavy. The waiting is the worst part. It feels the heaviest and the longest.

"I hate this part," I murmur and swallow thickly.

"It'll be over soon," Carter responds, neither of us daring to move even an inch.

"This is your last warning," the one cop calls through the speaker, and I'm all too aware that he's going to feel the need to call for backup. He has to know at this point that they should've never come here. Or maybe he believes the detective. That it's just an arrest and the other man is on their side.

There's only a small pang of guilt that flows through me as the cop door opens with the faintest click and the bang, bang, bang shoots out.

I turn in my seat, leaning out of the window and aim for the second cop, knowing my brothers have the others.

My body jolts and the world slows down as the bullets fly. The second cop ducks down in his seat while the window finally breaks from the relentless gunfire. The detective's car is fucked, popped tires and shattered glass.

In my periphery, I see the detective lifeless. He never had a chance. The first cop is in the driver's seat, the second still hidden but trapped.

Jase is faster than me and closer, striding up to the cop car and yanking the door open, a gun pointed at the cop's face. Daniel's on the other side of him and Carter and I make our way up to the car.

We have him surrounded. Jase removes the keys from the car, and the glass crunches under my feet as I walk up. Daniel reaches through the shattered window, opens the door from the inside and pulls the man out. He's dressed in his blues.

"Officer Angino didn't make it," I comment as I realize it's McKinley that's on his knees in the gravel road, begging for us not to kill him.

I swallow thickly, my finger on the trigger as my brothers wait silently. Not responding to the pleas echoing out into the cold night from the man. His breath turns to fog as he heaves in and out.

"You call for backup?" I question and McKinley looks at me a second too long, debating what answer to give me.

Bang! The gun kicks back in my hand and the poor bastard screams out, gripping his knee. Blood slips between his fingers as his shoulder slams into the gravel road and he crumples over.

"Don't lie to me," I tell him calmly as I bend down.

He pathetically attempts to hold back the tears of pain and shakes his head. His teeth bite down into his lip. I imagine right now every regret is piling up in the forefront of his mind.

"Look at me," I command and tap the gun against his cheek. The heat of it is searing and he bucks back.

"Do you have someone you love?" I ask him as he stares up at me. Wide-eyed, full of fear. He might be a prick but he's not dumb.

"He has a wife and kids," Daniel answers for him, crossing his wrists in front of him, gun still in hand. I look over at Jase and Carter, and Carter nods slightly.

"Tell me yes or no and they'll be safe. You understand. Either way, you answer, I end this quickly, and make sure no one touches them."

The poor bastard's face scrunches as he shakes his head in denial. As if he could wake himself up from this nightmare. But there is no way out of this life. He knows that. He made that choice.

"Nate, he's your informant?" I swallow thickly as he stares back.

"I'm going to raid your office, your everything, looking for all the evidence and proof. I'm going to find out some way and if your family is there...I'd prefer if you kept them safe by answering me."

Slowly he shakes his head. "We worked with your waitress, Scarlet. She said there was a guy who had intel and gave it to her. But I never spoke to him. Not once."

"Are there any other informants?"

"No," he shakes his head recklessly. "We were here for Nate. His connection was lost and we were told to get him out. That was it. That's all I know."

I nod, believing his panicked words as he pushes them out as quickly as he can. He peers up at me with a look in his eyes that tells me he's praying that I believe him. And I do. I already knew all of that, I just needed to hear it out loud. And Jase needed it recorded, so he can show it to the men, destroy it, and end the rumors.

"I'll keep my word. No one is going to harm your family, even though you all went after mine. I promise." He opens his mouth to say something but I put a bullet in it and then another in his skull. He falls backward in a thump and with that, I know this shit is over.

It's just a matter of cleaning up the scene, washing all this shit off me, and then climbing into bed with my wife.

CHAPTER 23

BRAELYNN

Seeing my mom at the Cross estate is something else.

My heart beats anxiously, and I can't stop watching her. Declan and his brothers don't know her like I do. I hope none of them can tell that her smile is forced and she's only being polite.

I can hardly keep track of the conversation before dinner. Aria, Carter, and Declan carry the chatter. Aria tries to draw my mom in, but she's been quiet, mostly just nodding and agreeing. As we take our seats, Aria brings a bottle of wine to the table and pours each of us a glass. Thank God. I desperately need it.

I focus on the wine spilling into the round bottoms of the glasses and breathe deep. It's always awkward, I remind myself. It would have been awkward at first even if Declan hadn't been a Cross and he'd asked me on a regular date. I would have been nervous bringing him home no matter what.

"We need a drink to cheers, I think," Aria says with a smile she gives each of us our glass. Carter and Declan have whiskey already so it's just the three of us women with prosecco.

The way Carter watches my mother reminds me of how he was when I first came here. He's a bit more reserved with my mom at the table. It occurs to me that he's always been guarded. His love for Aria slips out regardless.

He catches my eye, and I anticipate some kind of disappointment with how awkward this all is. Carter smiles instead, a genuine grin that creates a touch of wrinkles around his eyes. He lifts his glass in cheers toward me and I do the same.

Glasses clink and there's a bit of warmth that touches me. It's a feeling that's reminiscent of home.

My mother plays along respectfully but there's no smile on her face.

"Okay then." Aria takes her seat last, lifting her hands to indicate all the food on the table. "Let's eat."

She's made a full spread of Italian food. Bruschetta with fresh bread. Meatballs. Caprese salad. Creamy chicken and gnocchi. Handmade tortellini. It looks divine and smells even better.

Aria passes the first dish and smiles at my mother. "I'm

hoping there's something you'll like here," she says and then her eyes widen. "Oh! The lasagna." She jumps up from her seat and brings the last dish back to the table. All the while she's gone, it's quiet, apart from the clinking of serving spoons against the porcelain dishes.

"I salvaged it," Aria states, placing down the pan of homemade lasagna. "The one corner is a little less than perfect."

My mom speaks kindly and of her own free will for the first time, "If it tastes as good as it smells, I'm sure it's delicious." Her smile looks a bit more genuine, but it doesn't reach her eyes. She's skeptical. It's noticeable. Perhaps Aria is growing on her though.

Dinner continues with Aria mainly asking my mother questions and attempting to keep the conversation upbeat. All I can think is that my heart is breaking into two.

Declan finds my hand under the table and squeezes. He hasn't touched his drink. Neither have I.

Neither has my mother.

My mom stays quiet as we start eating. The conversation dims as forks clink against plates. Aria talks to Carter. Carter talks to Declan. Declan doesn't say anything to my mother, and she doesn't say anything to him. I keep glancing at him, begging him to say something to her but every vision of what he could say to her is not the man I know Declan to be.

I don't know how to make any of this right and I don't

know what to say.

The tension's obvious after a few minutes. I have to say *something.* Dinner with my own mother can't be like this. I can't sit at a table and pretend everything is fine when two people I love so dearly won't even speak to one another.

I've just opened my mouth to say something, anything, when Declan clears his throat.

"I love your daughter," he says, voice clear. "I wouldn't have married her if I didn't."

My mother's fork pauses midair and her eyes go wide as she stares at Declan for a long moment. Slowly, she lowers her fork and sets it on her plate. There's pain in her eyes when she speaks.

"Braelynn is my only child and my entire world—"

"Same for me," Declan says matter of factly, cutting her off. "It's a good thing that she has both of us to love her."

My mother swallows, and Carter and Aria sip from their drinks. I feel hot all over, on the verge of panic.

"I don't know when it happened," Declan continues. "But at some point, there was no turning back."

"In your life, there's hardly any going back. Isn't that right?" My mom's pushing him, and there are tears in her eyes. The emotion creeps into her tone and I imagine she's been on edge the entire night wanting to confront him. She knows enough that she should be scared I'm involved with him. I can't deny that.

"It's never too late for anything," Aria says, grabbing a piece of bread. "I don't know if you know this, Mrs. Lennox, but I grew up in this life, and I know how others feel about it. I know the hesitancy." Everyone at the table watches Aria now. "But I'm not in it any longer. I have children. I have my art, and I don't—" She licks her lips. "The brutality of it was too much."

"You are Aria Cross," my mother says in her best no-nonsense tone. "Of course you are in the life." My mom's voice doesn't shake, but she's about to cry. "I do not want this for my daughter."

"You don't want what, exactly?" Aria asks. Declan gazes at his hardly touched plate and squeezes my hand tighter. "There is no one who will love her more. No one who can give her more. She is family, which means you are as well."

Aria has a no-nonsense tone to rival my mother's and the tension at the table cracks.

"It may take time to adjust," Carter states, picking up his glass and taking a sip, "but I think the part where Declan really fucked up was keeping Braelynn to himself as they had their whirlwind romance."

He glances at my mother with sympathy. "He knows he shouldn't have. You can't blame him. He was the youngest and when our mom died, we didn't really baby him. He can be boneheaded sometimes."

I blink at Carter, barely recognizing his tone. He's almost...

charming as he placates my mother. A version of him I haven't met before.

Declan huffs a laugh at the description, although the emotion shows on his face. "I apologize, Mrs. Lennox," he says, looking her in the eyes, his own brimming with sincerity. "I have been selfish with your daughter and unkind to you. I will do better." My heart patters the softest beat, staring up at this man who could rule hell, as he apologizes to my mother and then rubs his thumb over my knuckles under the table.

My mother's silent. "We'll give you a key," Carter offers. My eyebrows must be up at my hairline, but he's not done speaking. "You can come over as often as you'd like and whenever you'd like."

"Unannounced?" my mother asks, obviously testing him, and I can't hold it in anymore. Declan and his family are being more than generous.

"Mama! You can't—"

"If you prefer to," continues Carter smoothly, stopping me from getting too worked up.

Before my mother can answer, Declan says, "I really am sorry. I wasn't thinking. I was only falling in love with your daughter. But she told me how much you mean to her, and I will never get between you two. Even if you worry, even if you never want me as a son—"

"I didn't say that," my mother says abruptly, and she has a look in her eye that's conflicted. I don't recognize this tone in her voice at first. She sounds almost like she's scolding him, but it's so soft that it can't be. My mother points a finger at Declan. "I didn't say that I don't want you as a son." She clears her throat and takes a sip of her drink. "I said I'm worried."

There's nothing Declan can say to that. We both know better than to think this world is completely safe for any of us. Life is not guaranteed, and especially not for anyone in the Cross brothers' lives. They're not the only ones like that, though. Danger can find a person anywhere.

"Time will be good for all of us, I think," Aria pipes up. For a minute I worry that my mom will argue with her or that she'll burst into tears at the table.

But my mother nods slowly and then tells them all she's thankful for tonight, and I can't help but smile.

All around the table, everyone picks up their forks again. The worst of the tension seems to have passed. In the new calm, I can see how it might be between all of us. I know Carter meant it when he offered my mother a key, and this... this could be a regular part of our reality. Dinners together. Getting used to each other. Getting to know each other as we actually are, not from the rumors and whispers that surround the Cross brothers.

After a moment of silence, my mother says, "Well," and Declan looks over at her, his eyebrows raised. "I know where you live now." She says it as if it's a real threat, her voice lowered and her eyes narrowed, and there's a moment of tense silence at the table.

Then she smiles to herself, and Carter laughs. Declan follows him a second later, and so does Aria. I can at least smile at that as more hope slips in.

I know in this moment that it's going to be okay. Aria's right. Time is going to be good for all of us. It will take time to figure out how we all fit into this life, but we *will* fit. I won't have it any other way. I'm going to have the people I love with me, even if it takes work.

The best things usually do, anyway.

After a few minutes, Aria starts telling Carter about a new painting she's working on, and I reach over for my mom's hand. For a second, all three of us are touching. I have her hand in mine, and Declan's hand covers mine under the table.

My mom looks me in the eyes, pride and patience on her face.

"We got started off on the wrong foot, Mama." My throat gets tight thinking of all I've been through since I met Declan Cross. Since before I met Declan, even. The two of us have come a long way, and my mom and I came even further together. "But I promise you, I'm happy. This is what I want."

"And I love her more than anything." Declan lifts my hand from beneath the table and kisses my knuckles. He rests our clasped hands on the table, no longer hiding it from my mother or from anyone.

My mom stares at our hands for a long moment, tears

glistening in her eyes. They don't fall, though. She raises her napkin from her lap and dabs at her eyes, taking a long, deep breath. Then she looks Declan in the eye. "You need to make me a promise."

He clears his throat, looking back at her. They're both very serious now. It's not a joke, and I know Declan can tell that as easily as I can. "What promise is that?" he asks.

"Promise me you won't let anything happen to her."

My mom doesn't have to make a threat along with her request. If anything were to happen to me, she would do whatever she could to get justice for me. But the truth is, none of that would matter to her. The only thing she's ever wanted is for me to be safe and happy. The stakes are higher than retribution and revenge. She's telling Declan, in not so many words, that her heart would be broken forever if any harm were to come to me.

My own heart skips a beat. At the very least, they understand each other, Declan and my mom, even if they don't realize it yet. They both love me more than anything else. It's something not everyone in the world gets to experience, being loved by two people like this. There have been times in my life that I thought I couldn't get any unluckier, but now it's crystal clear.

And that kind of love...that's a true gift. One that shouldn't ever be taken for granted.

I make my own silent promise to always, always remember

this moment. The serious way Declan looks at my mom, with the obvious desire for acceptance. The way she looks back at him, hopeful and trusting but knowing so much is out of her control. She wouldn't be here if she didn't want to give him a chance, and this question is the true test.

Because, of course, she can't keep me safe all on her own. She tried her best when I was a child, and now that I'm a grown woman, she has to do her best to trust other people, starting with my husband.

"Will you take my word for it?" Declan asks, his voice rough. I wonder if it bothers him to say this in front of Carter and Aria, but I don't think so. He hardly looks at them. He'd say this no matter who was in the room. That makes my heart even warmer.

My mother nods, accepting as solemnly as if they're making an eternal pact. I guess, in a way, they are.

"Then I give you my word," Declan says. "I swear to you. I won't let a damn thing happen to my wife. She'll be safe with me."

Chapter 24

Declan

I don't remember a time that I've been so damn nervous. I barely touched my plate and I don't trust the whiskey. All I can think as I stare across the table all night at Mrs. Lennox is that she reminds me so much of my own mother. Memories of my childhood play back as I sit there, scraping the fork across my plate.

I knew I wasn't good enough for Braelynn back then, and I'm sure as hell not good enough for her now.

Her mother knows that. It's so fucking obvious that her mother knows that. We all do.

But I can't let Braelynn go. I won't do it. I love her and I don't know how I could survive without her anymore.

With dinner and dessert done, her mother slips on her

coat. Hugs were given to all, including me, more than likely reluctantly. Carter and Aria have gone and as Braelynn's telling her to drive safe, Mrs. Lennox asks me for a private minute.

If I was nervous before, I have no fucking clue what this feeling is. The pit of my stomach twists and turns as I nod and Brae lets go of my hand to leave me alone in the foyer.

"Love you neña," she murmurs to her daughter who looks skeptically back as she walks to the kitchen to give us a moment.

Brae's footsteps can barely be heard when her mother tells me calmly, "I remember when you were a little boy, do you remember me?"

If only she knew.

I clear my throat, swallowing down the emotion, "I do." I wonder what she sees when she looks at me. I wonder if I look like a cold-hearted monster to her, because right now I feel the same as I did back before I knew what this world was.

She glances past me, holding her purse against her chest. "You're not so little anymore. Seems like a lot has changed."

"A lot has changed but I—" I breathe out deeply before meeting her gaze, "I loved her then. I just didn't know how much I needed her. I'm sorry I couldn't stay away from her." My voice cracks slightly, betraying me, and I hate it.

I clear my throat again as her mother eyes me. Perhaps thinking that I'm lying to her. And I suppose with all the lies I've told, I deserve that, but I can prove to her that I mean everything I say.

Her mother speaks just above her breath, "She deserves someone who loves her."

I don't hesitate to answer, "I do. I do love her. And I'll take care of her."

A moment passes and then she nods, as if accepting it, and for a moment, it feels like everything might be all right.

"I expect to have dinner every Sunday." I nod in return and tell her we can do that.

"Good," she says with finality and then looks behind her at the door. Before she leaves, she says, "Next week, dinner at my house." Again I nod. I would do anything for her. She adds, "Just you two or your family can come."

"They'll be there," I answer for my brothers, and then I think about all the kids and how I think her mother would love that.

"Just to warn you, it is a large family."

"Well that's just fine. I have a large table."

CHAPTER 25

BRAELYNN

My mom hasn't been gone for five minutes when she messages me.

He really loves you, the text reads. I smile at my phone and tap out my answer. *I know. And I love him too.*

I make my way to get a much-needed drink with Declan, my shoulders relaxed, my body light in a way it hasn't been in a long, long time. My life is coming together. My mom's part of everything again. She knows about Declan and our love. Maybe not everything, as there are certain things I'll never breathe life into again. And, for the first time, I feel like I'm right where I'm meant to be. Like this is the start of my forever.

With my thoughts getting ahead of me as I nibble on a bit

of chocolate cake, Carter and Declan walk into the kitchen. Mid conversation and for a moment I wonder if I should leave. I don't want to overhear anything—ever—that isn't for me to know.

I murmur after swallowing down a delicious morsel and make my way past the two of them. "Sorry. I was just coming to grab a bottle of wine."

I start to turn, but Declan's already at my side. He takes my elbow and pulls me into a hug, dropping a kiss to the top of my head. "It's fine, Brae. We were just talking about the investigation. It should be over now."

I swallow hard. "Were you?" I lean out around Declan's embrace and wave at Carter. "Hey, Carter."

"Hi," he says. "Nothing to worry about. If they had enough evidence, we would know."

"Is there anything that I should know that they have?" I ask and then I hate how I ask the question.

Declan chuckles rough and low, and Carter answers for the both of them. "All they have is a fire to put out."

"Literally," Declan adds, a grin catching at the corners of his mouth. He looks delighted to be telling me this. Almost like it's something funny that happened at the office. As if the Cross brothers could ever have a normal office job to come home and tell their wives about. "Explosives in an office. All the evidence is either damaged beyond repair or gone."

"There's nothing to hold up in court," Carter says softly.

"The judge on the case now is firmly in our pocket."

"Is this too much?" Declan asks when I go wide-eyed and quiet.

It takes a few beats to clear the tight feeling from my throat. "No, I want to know that it's over but I'm not sure I need to know anything else."

"It's over," Declan says and once again kisses my temple.

I lean my head against his chest and let him hold me. I listen to his heartbeat, steady and strong. This is all that's important in the world. My *husband*, with me. Nobody's after us... for the moment. It's not a very grandiose dream, but it's come true, and that's what counts.

Carter clears his throat, and I pick my head up to find him on his way out. "Congratulations, you two," he says over his shoulder.

"On what?" Declan asks.

"On your marriage."

"Thank you," I tell him, new happiness fluttering in my chest. This is when our real marriage starts, isn't it? No part of it has anything to do with staying safe from depositions or police. It's the two of us.

Declan put his hands under my chin and tips my face to his. He kisses me slow and soft, and I taste all the love he has for me on those lips. After a minute, he deepens the kiss, and just when I think he's going to lift me off my feet, he backs me into the counter instead.

I don't care at all if anyone else is going to walk in. I don't care that they could. I throw my arms around his neck and kiss him back, just as deep. If all this has taught me anything, it's that I'm never going to take a single second with Declan Cross for granted. I don't think I'll take a single second of anything for granted, but especially not with him.

He makes a low sound in the back of his throat and nips my bottom lip.

"My wife," he says, his tone hot and possessive. It makes me melt. So does the glint of the ring on my finger. Declan's voice is a private sign that I belong to him, but the ring? That's the public one. "Should we go back to the bedroom?"

I shake my head, smiling into the kiss. "No. I'm on my way to the wine cellar."

Declan groans. "I can't wait that long."

He picks me up in his arms, and I swat at him, nipping his bottom lip and tugging just slightly. The masculine rumble in his chest lights everything on fire inside of me.

Declan kisses me back and carries me to the wine cellar. In the polished room with the many, many bottles gleaming on their shelves, he kicks the door closed behind him and sets me on my feet.

Then his hands are all over me. They're under my dress, tugging my panties down. He manages to get both my shoes off in the same motion. I don't help him at all. I keep my hands in his hair as he kneels to slide the panties off, and then I drag him back up to kiss me again.

I'm desperate and needy, just like he is.

Declan carries me to a countertop in the back, my ass touching down on gleaming wood. He kisses me like I was gone for years, not just for a dinner, his hands exploring every part of me that he can reach. Fingers delve between my legs to toy with my clit and push inside me. When he discovers I'm very much ready for him, he groans again, directly into my mouth, and lifts his fingers to his mouth to suck off my arousal.

I thread my fingers together at the back of his neck and kiss him, stopping only to pull back so I can see his eyes. My heart races and my body heats as I stare into his wanton gaze. This is how much Declan wants me. This is how much he needs to be with me. He didn't even want to wait until I came back from the wine cellar. What would it have been, two minutes? Three? I wouldn't have taken long to pick out the wine with him waiting in the bedroom.

He reaches down for his belt and his zipper, and when he's freed himself, he takes my ass in his hands and pulls me to the edge of the counter. Declan pushes into me in one smooth stroke. He shudders as he sinks inside of me, covering my mouth with his again. From this angle, every thrust makes contact with my clit, and I know I'm going to find my release fast and hard. It's half from that contact, but the other half is just how much I want him.

Just how happy I am to be with him. Just how perfect it is now that we're okay. Now that we're free.

"Declan," I moan his name as the pleasure builds.

I hook my legs around him and dig my heels into his lower back, pulling him closer. He fucks me harder. It reminds me of the way he seemed when we first met. Strong and intimidating. He scared me. Now, the way he moves would be frightening if I didn't know him. All his energy and focus are on me.

He rocks my hips into him with his hands, grinding us close together, and I throw my head back. Pleasure builds and builds and builds until I'm not seeing the ceiling of the wine cellar anymore. I'm not seeing much of anything. I'm just feeling him there, his muscular body between my thighs.

Declan changes something about the way he's moving me, and the direct contact on my clit pushes me over the edge into a shaking orgasm.

"Good girl," I hear him say. It sounds like he's a million miles away, but it's just that there's so much pleasure. My heartbeat is so loud. "That's it."

He lets me ride it out, and then he's leaning over me, one hand braced on the countertop so he can fuck me as hard as he wants to. All I can do in the post-orgasm haze is hold on to him. With my body hot and the sweet mixture of pain and pleasure as he fucks me harder and harder, my neck arches and I cry out my pleasure.

I bite Declan's neck, then kiss the teeth marks, then lick my way up the side of his neck. When I reach his mouth, he kisses me with a grunt and comes hard, pinning me to him, letting the countertop balance the rest of my weight. Declan finishes with another shudder and presses another set of kisses to the side of my neck.

We both stay there for a minute, just breathing. Feeling the high slowly come back down together.

After he's caught his breath, Declan lifts me down from the countertop and smooths my dress into place. He runs his fingers through my hair, setting it in place again. When he's finished, his hands linger on my face. He looks into my eyes like he never wants to forget the color. I could never forget the color of his, no matter how long I lived. He murmurs, "You're mine."

"And you're mine," I say, hooking my finger into the collar of his shirt and tugging him in for a kiss. It's another slow, sweet one, and I know at this moment that I'll never be tired of kissing him. "I love you," I say when he pulls back. "I love you so much, Declan."

"I'll love you forever," he promises. Then he gives me one more kiss, straightens up, and takes my hand. "I will love you forever, Braelynn."

"Forever," I agree.

Epilogue

Braelynn

Three Months Later

I'm already in the office when Declan strides in, exuding nothing but confidence and power. My body tenses and I stir slightly, eager for what's to come.

His suit is perfectly fitted to him, custom and expensive, but it's the man underneath that gives them their appeal. He's all muscle, but the fire in his eyes says that physical strength is only a small part of his command.

He closes the door behind him and his eyes rake over me. My heart races as I reach for the pen and then drop it; I go still as his eyes meet mine.

"Braelynn." His voice is its own command.

"I—" I stand up, intending to say more, but he crosses the

room and pushes me back against the desk.

Declan kisses me hard, letting all his raw power filter through the kiss. He nips at my bottom lip, drags his teeth over my jaw, and bites at my shoulder. He pushes up under my skirt and he brushes his knuckles over my panties.

So much of this moment reminds me of how we started. My heart races as his dark eyes pierce mine with an intensity that shows me he feels the same. Only now, I am his completely and he is mine.

"Over here." Declan walks us over to the chair behind his desk and sits down. I'm more than willing to follow his lead and straddle him. I'm just as in need as he is. He's undone his belt and zipper with a rough hand, then he shoves my panties aside. "Be a good little whore for me."

With his hand gripping my hip and guiding me, I slide down onto him. My lips form a small "o" as he stretches and then fills me.

The sweet tinge of pain mixed with pleasure is everything I need and the heat engulfs my body. He lets me take my time at first, kissing along my neck.

"Harder," he pulls back and orders. Our gazes meet as he aids me in riding him harder and faster. My breasts bounce harder than before. He pulls at my blouse and a button pops. With a firm tug, he pulls a cup down to release my breast. His lips are on my nipple instantly. He sucks and nips, adding to my pleasure.

I lift up and stroke down on him, my hands braced on his shoulders and my nails digging into the fine fabric as the waves of pleasure crash down on me unexpectedly.

"Declan," I cry out his name as I come undone.

"Fuck yes," he growls in the crook of my neck as he pounds into me harder, leaning me back against the desk as he stands up straighter, riding through my orgasm recklessly. He takes over and I can barely control my strangled cries of pleasure.

Our warm breath mingles as our heavy breathing only adds to the intensity and he kisses me. I know he's close, and I can feel another impending orgasm as well.

As our hearts pound against one another, someone knocks at the door. Declan curses under his breath. It's not locked. They could just walk in and see us like this.

I wait for his command, very much still filled with his cock, "under the desk." Without hesitation, I slide off Declan's lap and onto my knees. Every inch of my skin is still sensitized and I've barely caught my breath.

Declan slides his chair in, his feet planted wide. I put my hands on his knees and look up at him. He doesn't look down at me as he calls, "Come in."

The door opens, and I wait a moment.

"Mr. Cross." It's one of the managers from the front of the house. I recognize his voice. A light tapping sound says he's got a notepad in one hand, and he's using the base of his pen to worry at it while he stands there.

Declan's dick is still hard, and he's still in need. He readjusts himself in his seat, and his hand rests on his thigh before his two fingers motions for me to come closer. I can still feel him inside of me, and the pleasure he's just given me urges me forward.

I take his cock in my hand and give it a gentle stroke, then a harder one. His breath hitches and I'm tempted to lean forward and lick. I let the tip of my tongue glide up his slit and his hand wraps around the back of my neck as the conversation continues.

"We're cutting it too close on the top-shelf spirits. What do you think about a 25 percent increase?"

"Hmm." There's no sign in Declan's voice that I have my fist wrapped around his cock. I give him another harder stroke, then inch myself up so I can better serve him orally. With his fingers firmly gripping my neck, he holds me still and I wait with baited breath. "When you say cutting it close, what do you mean, exactly?"

"I mean that twice last week we've had to run out mid-shift for more. It hasn't caused any problems, but if it happens on a busy night, we'll be down a server or a bartender."

"Is 25 percent more on the order enough to stop that from happening?"

"I think so. But it's also about timing. Shipments tend to come in a day after we've already had to go out for replacements."

The moment his grip loosens, I lean forward and close my lips around the head of Declan's dick, and the only sign he gives is that his thighs tense. His muscles tighten under my palms. I suck ever so gently and I've never felt so dirty and so powerful as he lets go of my neck and spears his fingers through my hair, letting me suck him off.

His voice tenses just slightly as he asks, "Any way to rework the shipments?"

"Delivery driver says no. I checked with him before I came down here. It would mean an extra fee if he had to make two trips to this area."

"Which costs less?" he asks quickly and beneath me, the heels of his shoes dig into the carpet. I hollow my cheeks and take more of his cock into my mouth, all the way to the back of my throat.

"Between the fee and the increased orders?"

"Yeah."

The manager consults his list, and it's silent for a minute. Declan's feet rise so his heels are two inches above the floor. I stop taking him deeper and concentrate on licking him, keeping my lips tight around his shaft. One of his heels taps three times in quick succession. His thigh trembles, just a little, and the silence seems to drag on and on and on.

"The fee is less, by a little. So..."

"So go with an increase in the order."

The manager laughs. "I thought you'd say just the

opposite." I pause, so I can readjust and get more comfortable.

"We can sell everything we order for the bar. We can't make any money off the fee." As he talks, I wrap my hand around the base of his cock and work him with both my hand and mouth. "So if the price is only a little different, it's obvious to me that the order should just increase to match our need."

Declan's voice catches, just a tiny bit, on the word *need*. And I fucking love it.

"Got it."

"Anything else?" he asks quickly; I have a feeling he's close.

"There was something—" The pen taps on the notepad again, and Declan presses his heel into the carpet hard. I can't do anything but add suction and tension to the blowjob, because the poor manager would know I was under here.

"No. I think that's all. I'll send an email with–"

"You do that," Declan cuts him off, "Close the door behind you on your way out."

"Yes, sir."

The door shuts a few long seconds later, and Declan pulls me up from under the desk and into his lap. "You wicked little thing." He runs his thumb over my now swollen lips with a devious look in his eyes and a hint of pride there too.

"I'm sorry," I murmur with a half smirk, unable to catch my breath.

Declan kisses me hard and pulls me over his lap, angling me onto his cock again. When I slide down onto him, taking all of him inside me, he lets out a deep groan. The pleasure is intense as I ride him slowly, the pleasure returning with a vengeance and threatening to overwhelm me.

"Declan, I...I don't know if—"

He takes me by the hips and makes me do it. I lose myself in the motions, focusing on holding on to him and enjoying this moment, reveling in his touch.

Declan's hand slides between us and he uses the pad of his thumb to rub at my clit. Slow circles at first, then faster, the pressure staying light and even. The orgasm starts to build in my toes and moves up through my legs, finally gathering under his thumb. Declan watches me like he's never seen me do this before, only he has. Plenty of times. He has me come on a daily basis. But his eyes are hot, filled with love and lust, and they stay firmly on my face as I fuck him harder and faster.

"That's it," he says. "You look so fucking good like this. Come on my cock, Braelynn."

"Someone could walk in," I manage to say, digging my nails into his shoulders.

"And then they'd see a man with his wife," he says, gruff and almost impatient. "They'd better see you coming on my cock."

That pushes me over, and I'm still riding the waves of pleasure when he captures my mouth with his and comes too. It's a long, pulsing orgasm. When it's over, Declan drops his head onto my shoulder and kisses up my neck, slow and sensual and a little teasing. "I love you, Braelynn."

As my heart pounds and the flush comes over me, I know he's telling me the truth and I respond with every bit of my heart and soul, "I love you too."

About the Author

Thank you so much for reading my romances. I'm just a stay at home Mom and an avid reader turned Author and I couldn't be happier.

I hope you love my books as much as I do!

More by Willow Winters
www.willowwinterswrites.com/books

This is the Discreet Edition so no-one knows what you are reading.

You can find each edition at

www.willowwinterswrites.com/books